SMASH YOUR HEAD
ON THE
PUNK ROCK

SMASH YOUR HEAD ON THE ON THE PUNK ROCK

MATT BISSONNETTE

Exile Editions

Publishers of singular
Fiction, Poetry, Drama, Non-fiction and Graphic Books

2007

Library and Archives Canada Cataloguing in Publication

Bissonnette, Matt
 Smash your head on the punk rock / Matt Bissonnette.

ISBN 978-1-55096-100-3

 I. Title.

PS8603.I88S53 2007   C813'.6   C2007-906539-2

Design and Composition by MPC Design
Cover Design by Ingrid Paulson
Original Artwork – "Dave" © 1997 – for Cover by Phil Grauer
Typeset in Stone Serif and Akzidenz Grotesk
Printed in Canada by Gauvin Imprimerie

The publisher would like to acknowledge the financial assistance of
the Canada Council for the Arts and the Ontario Arts Council, which is an
agency of the Government of Ontario.

Conseil des Arts   Canada Council   ONTARIO ARTS COUNCIL
du Canada   for the Arts   CONSEIL DES ARTS DE L'ONTARIO

Published in Canada in 2007 by Exile Editions Ltd.
144483 Southgate Road 14
General Delivery
Holstein, Ontario, N0G 2A0
info@exileeditions.com
www.ExileEditions.com

Canadian Sales Distribution: U.S. Sales Distribution:
McArthur & Company   Independent Publishers Group
c/o Harper Collins   814 North Franklin Street
1995 Markham Road   Chicago, IL 60610
Toronto, ON M1B 5M8   www.ipgbook.com
toll free: 1 800 387 0117   toll free: 1 800 888 4741

for
Molly

And what was it that I delighted in, but to love, and be loved? but I kept not the measure of my love, of mind to mind, friendship's bright boundary; but out of the muddy concupiscence of the flesh, and the bubblings of youth, mists fumed up which beclouded and overcast my heart . . .

—S. AUGUSTINE

THE WARM UP

Ryan Pearse standing on the corner with a hockey bag in his hand. The streetlights changed and then changed again. Ryan set his load down, took a seat on a bus-stop bench. From there he could see St. Kevin's. The rectory was behind the church. A few lonely snowflakes dribbled from the gutter slush sky. He looked up and down Sherbrooke Street. Then up and down Regent Avenue. Sherbrooke again. Then Regent. The clouds were such a sickly grey it was hard to tell where they ended and the grimy city began. Ryan picked his hockey bag back up, crossed Sherbrooke, and started down the path that ran along the side of St. Kevin's. Halfway there he saw Bug appear from around the far corner. Ryan's heart heaved up his throat. Broken glass filled his lungs. White heat crackled every nerve. He dove behind a bush. The branches poked. Everything was quiet except for the scraping of his breath, the rattle in his chest. Bug walked toward Ryan's hiding place puffing on a cigarette. Ryan's ears listened to Bug's feet scuff the sidewalk as he ambled by St. Kevin's without so much as a glance toward the bush. Ryan waited till he was out of sight, till lungs and heart settled, then hurried back onto the path and up to the rectory door. He pulled the key from under the mat and let himself in.

Dropping his equipment in the hall, he headed for the kitchen. He took a Coke out of the fridge and a pack of Pop-Tarts from the cupboard. In the living room the TV buzzed. Father Tom? he called. From the bedroom at the end of the long hall came the reply, I'll be with you in a minute. Ryan sat down on the couch and looked at the TV: golf. Above the box hung a large picture of Jesus looking out over the room. Ryan turned to the small bookshelf beside the couch. It was filled with hockey almanacs and various religious writings. On the bottom shelf there was a pile of magazines, LIFE on top. He pulled Penthouse November 1976 from the middle of the stack. Flipped it open to the centre. Miss November was lying in a pile of hay. She was wearing a red&white check shirt knotted at the waist and a pair of cut-offs. Her brown hair was piled in a bowl of messy curls on her head. On the next page she was naked, big tits and beautiful legs. Miss November was tanned dark brown except for breasts and ass that glowed snow white.

When he heard Father Tom coming down the hall he slid the magazine back in place. Why hello there Ryan, said Father Tom as he walked into the room. He was adjusting his priest's collar. Over that he had the cardigan and gray flannels he wore on game days.

– Hey Father Tom, said Ryan and then, how about LaFleur's goal last night. Did you see that?

– Did I see it? I was there.

– Really?

– I certainly was. The seats were right behind the Canadiens bench. Next time I get those tickets I'll take you.

Father Tom looked in the mirror making sure his collar was in place. He picked up his cup of coffee and took a sip. Then he said, Yes, that was quite a game. Almost reminded me of the old team, the passing, the skating. You don't see much of that any more. Now all we have is over-paid playboys.

– Things aren't what they used to be, Ryan agreed.

– Now that's the truth, said Father Tom, the gospel truth. With that decided he came and sat down on the couch. He crossed one leg over the other and then began in a very serious manner, We've got a big game ourselves this afternoon. If we win, we set the tone for the rest of the season. Beginnings Ryan, informed Father Tom, are very, very important. Start off on the right foot, and you end up in the right place. Get that first goal, win that first game, your job is half done.

Ryan took a sip of Coke and nodded his head. The Maroons are a pretty good team, he answered, that kid Langley can really skate.

– Yes he can, agreed Father Tom, and he can put the puck in the net. The boy has good hands. And they've got ten more like him on the bench. Those Maroons have depth and fire power. Sweet Mary and Joseph do they ever. That's why this game all comes down to you, Ryan. I don't want to put too much pressure on a boy your age, but you are the key to our defense. And defense is going to win or lose this game for us.

– There aren't many boys who could shoulder the challenge, Father Tom continued, to do that you need character. Character Ryan, that's what the great ones had, the Rocket, Doug Harvey, Jean Beliveau. All character players, top to bottom. All professionals, real pros. Not like we have today.

– You've got to be at the top of your game this afternoon, he kept on, completely focused, total concentration. One hundred and ten percent. That's the key, said Father Tom and he rumpled Ryan's hair. Then he added, but sometimes even that's not enough. There is something for you in the other room that I think will help.

– What is it? asked Ryan.

– Go see for yourself, son.

Ryan walked down the hall. Past the dining room, the study, the bathroom, to the bedroom, furnished with an old wood desk, a chair, a bed, the ubiquitous cross and companion. There on the bed was a new pair of hockey gloves. Ryan picked them up. They were beautiful. Well padded. All leather. Reinforced palms. Red, white and blue. Habs' colours. He rolled them over in his hands. Do you like them? asked a voice. Ryan looked up. Miss November was standing in the doorway. Sure, he answered. Miss November walked into the room. Long tanned legs. Golden hairs on her belly. I'm glad you like them, she said. She knelt down in front of him. Ryan closed his eyes. He thought about her big round tits. Miss November fumbled with his jeans. He thought about her nipples. Puffy brown. He felt her old, rough hands on his thighs, tugging at his underwear, pulling out his cock. Miss November's breath was coming in jerky rasps, like a car's engine on a winter morning. He though about her pussy. The tan lines, and the way her hair was shaved into a diamond. Her callused, gnarled fingers gave his cock a few quick yanks, cajoling it to attention. He thought about her ass, and the straw in her hair. From her painted mouth a deep voice croaked, oh my boy, my beautiful, beautiful boy, and then it started to blow.

MONTREAL
Rehearsal space

Five a.m. and I'm packing the gear. Alone. Wrapping lead cords. Breaking down drums. Tucking amp heads and guitars into cases. After everything is loaded into the van I go back for a dummy check because it's sort of embarrassing if you drive five hundred miles and discover you're missing a pedal, a floor tom, a guitar, a bass player. Seems like I've got it all, though to be honest, it would serve those bastards right if something did get left behind, making me pack the gear alone. That's not very punk. Turn the lights out and the jam space settles into darkness.

THE TRICK

Ryan was in the cloakroom putting on his jean jacket. Bug was standing beside him. Henry says the new kid's got a trick, went Bug as he pulled his jean jacket off its hook and slipped his arms into the sleeves. What is it? asked Ryan. I don't know, said Bug, Henry didn't tell me.

Out on the playground kids were running all over the place, kicking footballs, playing tag, yelling, throwing things. Ryan and Bug drifted toward the champ squares where Stephen and Henry were deeply involved in a game, trading spinners and fakesies, super babies and the terrifying grand slam. After watching for a bit Ryan broached the subject, Bug says you said the new kid's got a trick.

– Yeah, that's what he said, answered Henry though all his attention had remained focused on the bouncing tennis ball that was batted by hand from square to square to square to square.

– So, what is it?

– Don't know, he wouldn't tell.

– What?

– He just walked up. Said I've got a trick. Then wouldn't tell me what.

– He wouldn't tell you? went Ryan, but he's a new kid.

– I know, but he still wouldn't tell me. Says you have to see it to get it. Till then it's secret, and with that Henry unleashed a super grand slam that sent the ball halfway across the schoolyard. They watched it go then turned back to each other. Let's go see this trick, said Ryan.

The boys started looking around for the new kid. They looked by the bottom of the steps where the pipes are; behind the trees and the bushes near the big fence; in the little kid's fort; they were thinking of going to the library when Henry said, There he is! And there he was, over by the small fence, throwing rocks into a metal garbage can. But just then the recess bell went and Mr. Russel was shouting: Get in line. Boys on the left. Girls on the right. Quiet everyone. Shuffling their feet, the boys lined up.

The next subject was Canadian History with Mrs. Vineberg. Stephen was sitting beside Ryan. Bug was behind, with Henry on the other side. As Mrs. Vineberg talked and talked about the fur trade, they looked at the new kid. He was sitting in the front row. Bug recalled that they had never paid much attention to this new kid. For starters, he wasn't good at sports, his haircut was dumb, and he wore those light blue North Stars; plus, when he talked, everything he said was stupid. Like on the first day, in his class introduction, when he said that his dad was a scientist who worked for the space program; that he used to live at Cape Cana-veral; and, that he was really good at surfing, so good that he had won trophies and even been in magazines: This chubby kid! With the light blue North Stars! A surfer! In magazines! With trophies! And then later, that very same day, after Fiona Reed had peed her pants, he put his hand up and made a big deal about it, though he'd only been in their school less than a day, and everyone had known Fiona since forever. There and then they had sized the new kid up, and forgotten all about him. But now, now there was this trick.

At lunch they cornered the new kid. He was sitting by himself in the lunchroom playing electronic football. Bug, Ryan, Henry and Stephen walked up to this table. They looked down at him. He looked up at them.

– They want to know about your trick, said Henry.

– What trick?

– The trick you told me about.

– I didn't tell you about any trick. Henry turned to his friends, He did so say he had a trick. Henry turned back to the new kid, You fucking liar, you know you said it.

– Did not.

– Did too. Henry grabbed the new kid and put him in a head-lock. You said you had a trick!

– No.

– Yes. Henry squeezed harder. The new kid's chubby face turned bright red. You weren't supposed to tell anyone, said the new kid.

– Tell them about what?

– Nothing.

– About what?

– The trick, squawked the new kid. Henry let the new kid go. Again he turned to his friends. See? he said smiling. The new kid was in his seat coughing. So what's the trick, asked Ryan. The new kid didn't say anything.

– Come on, what is it?

– I just can't tell you. You have to see it. And I don't like to show a lot of people.

– If you show us then we'll all go to Stephen's after. He's got a big TV and tons of good food, promised Ryan. The new kid sat still for a moment. They all looked at him. The new kid wiped his nose. Just you guys? he asked.

The boys agreed that the basement bathroom was the place for the trick. The basement bathroom was safe. It was where they went with Frances to fuck. Though they didn't actually fuck. For the most part, a boy would go in the stall, and Frances would let him touch her tits and ass. Sometimes she would rub a cock for a bit, and maybe it got hard, but not a lot else happened. Though there was one time when Henry was in the stall and Bug pushed open the door. Henry was down on his knees and he was licking Frances's ass. They all really laughed about that: Henry Asslicker! But Frances got mad and wouldn't come down to the basement for a while. So they all agreed not to open the stall anymore. It was funny, but they knew they had a good thing going. They knew better than to mess it up.

All afternoon the boys wondered about the trick. They passed notes back and forth asking what could it be? They thought and thought, recalled tricks they had seen, things kids did to their eyes and mouths and tongues that made them look weird, routines done with yo-yos or other toys. Bug remembered a magic show he'd seen on TV. A magician had tricks with cards and coins and a hat. Was the new kid the kind of kid who did magic? Who spent a lot of time at home pulling rings apart, making his dad's handkerchiefs disappear? That was probably it. Yeah. Probably. But was it? Was it? As they wondered the afternoon dragged on. Weak autumn sun shone on the empty schoolyard.

Finally the last bell rang. They raced through halls clogged with kids. Down in the bathroom they sat on the ledge by the window to wait. Five minutes later the new kid showed. He walked in and looked at them. What's she doing here, he said pointing to Frances who was sitting on the ledge with the boys. She's allowed, she's part of our club, said Ryan.

– No way. No girls, said the new kid.

– She's part of the club, said Ryan.

– No, I can't do it with a girl.

– Oh yes you can, said Henry and he got up and started toward the new kid, curling his hands into fists. Ryan headed him off. This is bullshit, said Henry from behind Ryan, you tell us all about this big trick, and we wait all day, and then you won't even do it! If it's such a big secret, why'd you go telling me about it in the first place!

– You have to let me join your club, said the new kid.

– Join our club? said Henry, You? Join our club? First of all . . . Ryan quickly interrupted and told the new kid that sure, sure, sure he could be in the club. Then he turned to all of them and said, if he does the trick, then he can be in our club, OK?

The five sat on the ledge. The new kid stood by the wall, near the sinks. He took off his knapsack, and then he undid his pants. He leaned over till he was almost bent in two. What the hell? asked Henry.

– I think he's sucking it, answered Frances.

– Yeah, you're right, said Bug, he is sucking it.

– Oh shit, from Stephen.

– Holy fuck, Ryan confirmed. They stepped closer for a better look. Sure enough the new kid had his cock in his mouth and was sucking it. At a loss for more words, the kids just stared. Then the new kid stopped. He pulled his pants back up. They looked at him. He looked at them. That's it, said the new kid, that's the trick, so I'm in the club now, right? Oh sure, answered Ryan. The new kid started to smile. Sure, you're in the club, Ryan smiled back furiously, you big stupid faggot. And he pushed the new kid against the wall. And Henry socked him hard in the stomach. And then they stuffed him in the garbage can. Welcome to the club . . . ha . . . ha ha . . . ha ha ha . . .ha ha haha ha ha ha . . . ha . . . ha . . . . ha.

On the way to Stephen's house they were all still laugh laugh laughing about the new kid, and the trick, and the garbage can, and there was no club, and what a gaylord, but the laughter was a little too hard, and their tiny hearts and stomachs felt cold and empty, and the leaves were blowing down the street, and as they cut through the park snowflakes started to sprinkle so they buttoned their jean jackets tight and started walking a little faster, puffing on their cigarettes a bit harder, small fingers turning white blue in the cold.

They stopped by the outdoor rink and huddled out of the wind behind the boards, which were already up, though the ground still hadn't been flooded with water, so dead grass was stretched out where ice should have gleamed. They talked about hockey, in particular the Habs' start this year . . . 11-2 . . . best October in four years . . . they ought to make it easier on everyone, just give us the Cup now . . . while smoking a hash joint that Frances' old – that is to say, from the days Frances needed one –

babysitter had given her. Almost everyone agreed that Frances' old babysitter – named Julie Cobb, and now at the high school in the ninth grade – was totally hot, except, of course, Frances, who rolled her eyes, and said things like: as if she would even *think* about any of you losers, to which the boys replied with things like: oh, that's funny, because I just fucked her, in the ass, twice. The wind rattled the tree's naked branches, and if you were high enough on hashish they seemed to be scratching the bellies of the big brown clouds that were rolling in.

Down in the warm basement, they smoked more cigarettes – Stephen's parents still at work, and his mom a smoker, so the tobacco smell almost a family member, unlike, say, hash – ate oatmeal cookies and drank cups of hot tea laced with heaps of milk and sugar. They argued about which of the Rock Gods to put on: Sweet's *Fox On The Run* (Henry hates), anything off of Bowie's *Changes* (Stephen *so* bored with), *Not Fragile* by the Bachman Turner Overdrive (and vetoed by Frances), Rolling Stones (no), The Who (no), Led Zeppelin (no), until Bug said, well fuck then, what about this, holding up Queen's *A Day At The Races*, which prompted Henry to throw a shoe at him, grab Kiss *Destroyer*, and announce: This is it!

Henry marched over to the turntable, but there was already an album on. He picked it up, looked at the yellow Sire label, and then asked Stephen, hey, who the hell are the Ramones? Must be, according to Stephen, some weird record that belonged to his older brother Richard, a mysterious person who once lived up on the third floor, but had now gone to a far, far away land called University of Michigan, though was home last weekend for Canadian Thanksgiving. They passed round the jacket and looked at the four weird guys in the crumby b&w photo, leaning against a brick wall, all dressed the crumby same: Way-outs' (Flintstone variety) haircuts, ripped jeans, beat-up old Gilligan (of the island) tennis shoes, black leather jackets, tight, tight t-shirts. And all at once, all together, they are all yelling, Put it on! Put it on! Put it on! . . . a switch is pulled, a needle hits home, and you and your friends are hearing some sounds coming out of some speakers, staring at some record jacket, watching some vinyl spin, and every secret hope you never told a soul is finally coming true for you and your friends are falling in love for the very first time in some basement listening to some band and believing for some two minutes and thirty-seven seconds that some worms, like you, and yes, maybe even your friends, make it to butterflies.

OTTAWA
Barrymore's

This club is shit. I don't care what anyone says. People think it's great because it has movie theater seats and a big stage. But it's not. It's shit. The sound is shit, the lights are shit, the security is shit and they never give us enough beer. From our shit dressing room we can hear the opening band play. And they're shit too. Just kidding. They're not so bad, four young kids, and they seem to mean it, bashing through their last song, and then we're up. I take my place at the side of the stage, while the band picks up their gear. The first chord rings out and everyone starts to jump up and down. Guitars going clang. Kids setting off like roman candles. Even I'm up on my feet yelling like a young one. Then half way through the third song I can feel them stumble. Air hissing out of a balloon. Water down a drain. And it's gone. The night continues on, but it is over. They were never the tightest, never liked to practice all that much, it was part of their charm, but this is ridiculous. None of the kids seem to notice though, except when Tim stops playing drums for the last two songs and does jumping jacks instead, that is pretty hard to miss. Back in the dressing room it's awfully quiet. Band knows they played shit, and are sitting around sheepish, as they should. In the van it isn't any better. Tim behind the wheel with me in the navigator seat. Chuck in back on the bench with Sara and Phil on either side of him. None of them saying anything. I put in my Ultra-Core mixed tape, and no one even cracks a smile. After a long minute Phil says, Come on Bug, turn that noise off. And I do. And we drive in silence. And things are bad. First night and already things are bad.

THE FIELD TRIP

Stephen can't believe he got talked into this. How did that happen? And with Henry, of all people. He turns and asks, how did this happen? What are you talking about? Henry replies. Are you sure you know these guys? Sure, I'm sure, Henry says, everyone knows the Ghost Ryders. Why are they called the Ghost Ryders? inquires Stephen. Don't know, says Henry, but you better not ask them because this one kid asked if it was 'cause they had no motorcycles and got punched right in his face. Really? Really, Henry confirms, happened in the arcade I saw the whole thing the kid was knocked clean out the guy just went back to his game, Joust, I believe. They walk on Stephen mulling that one over. Through Atwater Park they go, then along beside the Forum toward the Clay Oven. Stephen wonders aloud, say Henry why do the call it the Clay Oven? No idea, his friend explains. But you've been there before, Stephen checks. Oh yeah, tons of times, comforts Henry.

Ryan's mom is smoking a cigarette and stirring the porridge. She looks so young and pretty to Ryan who is at the table eating a piece of toast. She brings the porridge over then looks at the clock. Shit, I'm going to be late. Mom, this porridge is too hot, he answers, can I have some milk? Used the last of it for the coffees, she says, here, try an ice-cube, and as she puts one into his porridge. Ryan wants to know: MOM, MOM, WHAT THE HELL

ARE YOU DOING? Relax, just cooling it down, that's the way your father used to do it. Like that's a good reason, he says and they both have a ha ha warm family laugh. As she leaves she calls, don't be late for school. OK, he answers. The slam of the door. Ryan sips his coffee, opens the paper.

OK Mom, thinks Bug, hurry up . . . let's go . . . I can't believe she is still in her room getting dressed! It's almost nine! Mom, he yells, you're going to be late! She comes hurrying into the kitchen, how do I look? she asks. Great Mom, you look great, he tells her. It's not too much? she asks. No, it's perfect. OK then, and she comes gives him a kiss. You better hurry too, she says, or you'll be late for school. Soon as I finish breakfast, most important meal of the day, answers Bug. The door closes behind her. Fucking, he sighs, finally.

Frances' mom is about to let her off right in front of school so she asks, can you drop me at the corner? Why? her mom wants to know. I want to buy some gum at Mildred's, says Frances, the chewing helps me concentrate. So they stop at the corner. Have a good day. Frances leans in and gives a kiss, you too Mom. Inside Mildred's she orders a coffee and takes a seat near the back.

It was right not to tell Stephen, reasons Henry, as he can be such a whiny fuck in the ass, but I don't really know any of these guys, never really been to the Oven before, though Floyd Paterson told me it was a breeze, you just walk up to the bartender and ask for the purple micro-dot. Just be cool, he said.

Ryan rings the buzzer but when the answer comes can't tell if it's Bug or his mom or whoever so he screams loud into the speaker, PIZZA? . . . YOU ORDER A PIZZA? Bug says, shut up retard, and buzzes him in. Opening the door he asks, what is your problem? My cock is too big, answers Ryan as they walk into the living room where there is a lovely jug of red waiting on the coffee table. Oh, you too, says Bug who already has a glass going so he pours Ryan one and they toast to their two too big cocks, then light up . . . ahh . . . first smoke of the day, goes Bug, you just can't beat it. Ryan downs his glass, savoring the tooth-paste wine mingle, and listens as his friend starts talking about how it is weird since him and his Mom moved in here, the two of them, living in this small apartment. Bug's dad sold office stationery, used to go away on business, and last time he just didn't come back, apparently had another wife in some far off exotic place, Malaysia or perhaps Arizona. On top of that, he mortgaged the house, sold the car, and left many other debts, so Bug's mom had to sell what was left, move them here, and go work as a secretary at some fancy law firm. Don't worry about it Bobby, Ryan tells him – Bug's real name being Bobby, though the kids call him Bug on account of his youthful insect-collecting obsessions: ant farms, butterflies on pins, bottles of fireflies, pray-ing mantis in an aquarium, etcetera – then continues on, ex-plaining about his own father, how he forgets birthdays,

Christmases, to send the child support, and so his mom cries at the kitchen table because she can't pay the rent, all by way of saying don't worry about it too much, it's not you, that's just the way dads are, better get used to it, because, moms aside, no one, and I mean no one, gives a fuck . . . and on the TV there is a morning aerobics show, and all the girls are pretty, and it's all getting a bit too heavy, so the two friends move the discussion to having sex with them, and how wonderful that would be, but deep down Ryan can tell they are both still kind of depressed.

Stephen replays it again, thinking of how he will tell it, even as his legs and arms pump pump pump, thinking he will probably tell it something like Henry the fucking idiot goes right up to the bartender, total Hell's Angels looking guy and says, I'd like to buy some purple micro-dot, and the bartender says, what the fuck did you say to me kid? And so the fucking idiot says, I would like to buy some purple micro-dot, real slow like he is talking to a deaf dog, and the bartender says, get the fuck out of my bar. And so the fucking idiot says real loud: COME ON MAN, JUST SELL US SOME ACID! Then the bartender, with baseball bat, starts coming around the bar so the fucking idiot and me we have to haul ass.

Frances walks in and sees they are watching an aerobics show already well into the cheap grocery store wine they love so. She sits down and asks, what's this? Bug's favourite show, answers Ryan. Bug claims, no way, not my favourite, though I would like to fuck her. And her. And her. And her. Do we always have to talk about who you want to fuck, asks Frances, isn't there something else we could talk about? A moment's silence. Then Bug answers, no, and that gets the big laugh. Dicks, she calls them. Have a drink, counters Ryan. It's a bit early and that stuff is disgusting. My mom's got valium, offers Bug. So Bug passes out the little pink triangles and Ryan pours them all drinks and Frances decides why not.

Drifting through the beat chrome and glass of the Alexis Nihon Plaza Stephen is giving what seems to Henry like the hardest of times saying, been there a million times before, know everyone, a real fucking regular you are, all very sarcastic-like and, it seems to Henry, rubbing it in just a bit too much. OK, OK, Henry interrupts, so maybe I've never been there before, and maybe I don't know those guys, but we still don't have any acid, and that's the real problem now, so I suggest that instead of blaming people we work on the real problem. Real problem? yells Stephen, real problem?! Henry watches his eyes screw up behind standard gold framed glasses, his head threaten to pop off his skinny neck, his mouth spit, the real problem is you are a fucking idiot that almost got us killed! Shut the fuck up, Henry yells back. No, you shut the fuck up, screams Stephen, we're going over to Bug's now, I'm sick of this. Henry loudly maintains they are not going anywhere till they find some acid. Our friends are counting on us, and we are not going to let them down. This prompts Stephen to call him a fucking idiot again, and Henry is getting pretty tired of him saying that, and is letting him know, when this scraggy hippy slides up and says, couldn't help overhearing you boys might want to score. Stephen and Henry both stop yelling and look at the guy. Maybe, they say.

Frances is lying on the floor staring at the ceiling. Bug puts on the first Velvets album and everything is lovely. She lights a cigarette, and thinks cigarettes taste so good, thinks I love smoking. Henry and Stephen just showed up and are in the kitchen getting something to eat. Ryan is stretched across the couch transfixed by a man in a silver suit doing battle with a flying monster in the middle of Tokyo. Bug sits down beside Frances on the floor. He has been talking about his mother saying since she went back to work all her clothes have been getting shorter and smaller, and she is wearing tons of make-up, and then the other day I came home and there was a man . . . in the apartment! Frances thinks it's funny the way Bug says "man", like it was a lion or a tiger or something you could never imagine being inside an apartment. She tells him, that's so cool, your mom is a woman, with female needs, you should be so happy for her. Bug says, oh come on, don't say that about my mom. Henry, standing in the kitchen doorway with a mouthful of frozen waffle, points and says, Bug's mom has female needs! and then he laughs and laughs and laughs.

They drop the acid just before eleven. It's the first time for everyone, except for Henry who claims he tripped with Floyd Paterson a bunch of times last summer so really, thinks Stephen, it's the first time for everybody. Henry pops his like nothing, though that Stephen continues to himself, is probably just for show. Feeling a little uptight he waits, watches the other three, all warm and fuzzy from the V&V, giggle as they put the little tabs in their mouths, and so then so does he. Frances falls on the couch, Henry sits down beside her, and they start touching right there, which sparks a up chorus: Hey, Come On, Get A Room. So Henry asks, can we relax in your mom's for a bit? Sure, Bug says, just don't make a mess. Henry says, the way your mom's been putting out lately who's gonna notice? Bug throws a pillow as Henry slips through the door.

Ryan asks, do you feel anything? No, not yet, says Stephen. Hey Bug, he continues, Bug, do you feel anything? But Bug is over by the stereo putting on *Never Mind The Bollocks* sixth song first side *God Save The Queen*, turns it up real loud and with a tea-towel tied on top of his head Steve Jones-style he jumps up on the couch and starts the air guitar declaring, sod you wankers. Ryan jumps right up there with him, twisting his face into a fairly decent *We Mean It Maaann*! Great, thinks Stephen, so I get to choose between Paul and Sid, the drummer or the junkie, well forget being the drummer, so he starts stumbling, and they are all jumping around when the coolest thing happens one minute bouncing on the sofa with brooms the next it is like them really rocking the music out of them filling the room filling everything and they are rocking out rocking out rocking out rocking Bug thinking out this is it this is fucking it this is the best the absolute fucking best . . .

. . . OK, look there is no way I'm having sex with you, Frances answers, not with those guys in the next room. Come on, says Henry, it'll be fun. No, she counters, it won't be fun. Henry starts to beg, please Frances, please . . . please. It's so pathetic that she gives him a handjob to keep the quiet, but midway begins to enjoy watching him jerk as she tugs, oh oh, almost there, but no not quite yet, you wait a minute longer my little friend, just one little more, then Henry's cum jumps all over her hand. Just wipe it on the bedspread. Not on Bug's mom's bed, and she goes to the bathroom to wash. Standing in front of the mirror it looks like hot and cold rivers are running through her. She looks at her hand and the cum so white and shiny she puts it to her mouth and has a small taste, looking at herself in the mirror the cum on her tongue the feeling of spring in her mouth and she is strong like a train leaving. Back in the living room Frances watches boys jumping on the sofa singing No Future No Future No Future No Future No Future No Future as they go up and down and up and down knocking each other over from couch to chair to table to couch to chair to table to couch to chair . . .

. . . creeping down hallways in underwear heading for the pool when Henry opens this door and before they know it they are on the roof and Ryan looks out and it's tooooooo crazy the whole city laid out before him he can see the Mountain and the Cross and the Big O and it is just too fucking much and it is just too fucking cool and it just makes him want to drop another hit but he is so high now how high would he be then over there is a big vent for air-conditioning or who knows but it is spilling out these huge clouds filling the roof so Bug walks into it and they can't see him WE CAN'T SEE HIM he is in there so long then all of a sudden comes walking out like some kind of crazy alien but only wearing his boxer shorts so though they're really shivering now everyone has to try it Stephen says it's like I'm arriving here for the very first time after he walks out and that Ryan thinks is exactly it that is EXACTLY FUCKING IT like you are walking into this for the very first time skin feels so new Stephen so smart but then they are really cold so Ryan puts his hand on the door and IT WON'T OPEN they are out on the roof it is December there is snow on the ground snow on the roof snow on everything snow they are in their underwear and WE ARE GOING TO DIE explodes in Ryan's head like a GOING TO DIE and they all just stand there in the terror in eyes and Ryan says WE ARE GOING TO DIE and Bug tries the door for no reason because it is locked it is fucking locked man fucking the door opens and Ryan says, oh, sorry about that you guys . . .

. . . sitting in the deck chair Stephen sees is that father is he looking at me in his head Stephen asks is that father is he talking in my head talking your poor mother did not bring you into this world to take drugs jump in swimming pools with hoodlum friends we survived wars oceans locust and you what have you accomplished nothing you are nothing nothing boy nothing what have you done with your what have you done what have you Stephen closes his eyes looks again father is gone Henry there instead and Henry hey do you have a cigarette man oh man I need a do I need a cigarette . . .

. . . over by the diving board Frances peels off her t-shirt stands up on the board spreads her arms tits look so good to Bug bouncing hard nipples make him think of apples and Jell-o her stomach clean and smooth and tiny white wet panties so her pussy you can practically see her pussy looks over at Ryan and he is staring so is Stephen so is Henry and so they look at Frances up on the diving board and she looks down at them her back so straight and so strong like a queen like she waits they watch she waits just the sound of the water in the pool then two quick steps the board bends and arms, tits, stomach, pussy, legs slip into liquid. . .

. . . naked and wet wandering halls why can't we Bug wonders find the goddamn elevator it was just here where the hell did it go where did it . . . Oh hey, don't ring that bell! Jesus fuck Christ Ryan! I fucking have to live here my mom will cook my ass if she finds out the janitor is probably around hey doesn't the carpet feel funny under your feet like walking on mini-putt I think it's down this way come on you guys come let's get back to my place dry off get some clothes . . . Henry! Put that fire extinguisher down! Put it down! Holy fuck! Ryan! don't . . . please . . . don't . . . oh my shit . . . both of you cock-fuckers stop . . . stop stop stop . . . come on come on let's get the fuck out of here before the janitor shows up . . . please you guys . . . please . . . please . . . aww . . .

. . . this stuff is probably totally toxic I'm taking a shower wash-ing it off you boys should too, says Frances, oh for sure we will, says Henry standing dripping in the kitchen, oh yeah, they all say laugh covered in bits of white foam and Ryan who is looking through the fridge comes up with a bag of frozen cauliflower asks Bug, what the fuck is this looks like little brains, before swinging the bag hitting Henry so hard so Stephen laughs so hard he spits his drink across the kitchen sticky Coke all over the floor wall and Frances and ha ha ha OK, she says, I'm definitely taking that shower now . . .

. . . Stephen asks Frances asks Henry asks Bug asks Ryan asks Stephen and it is no no no no no no no cigarettes no one nowhere has none so they are soon moving along Sherbrooke down Regent in a funny dumb falling pack, laughing, tripping, pushing as they pass by St. Kevin's of all of a sudden Ryan feels his pants off feels Father Tom doing his things feels everyone watches everyone points everyone so disgusted and so Ryan SO DISGUSTING SO BAD SO SICK SO WEAK SO WHITE HOT DEATH SKULL MAGGOTS DISEASE HORROR OH THE MOTHERFUCKING HORROR SHAME OH THE MOTHER-FUCKING SHAME SO DIE RYAN DIE so pick up a rock and it flies at the church rock goes right through the stain-glass window and they all go, holy fuck! and run run run run run run run . . .

. . . that was so fucking stupid! says Henry and, what the fuck is wrong with you! but Ryan just says, don't know nothing, laughs shakes his head, you have a serious problem, Henry tells him, you are fucked up! cops are going to be coming for sure! that window cost a lot of money for sure! and it was part of the church! you can't throw rocks at the church! Fuck the church, Ryan laugh shakes again. Oh my god don't say that now we are cursed and now have to get back to Bug's right now! the cops! come on! the cops! but Stephen says, I don't see any police and we still need cigarettes. No, we need to get the fuck back to Bug's before we run into some cops, but everyone wants cigarettes so they head to the store still this according to Henry is a bad idea, a really bad idea . . .

. . . standing by the cash register everyone is going through their pockets to buy as many packs of smokes as they can because after this they are never going outside ever again Bug pulling out a few crumpled notes some change lint when all of a sudden Ryan pick up two big bags of chips and takes off out the door the lady behind the counter grabs a broom and starts out after him and the door is still open so they follow Ryan and the lady out and watch as down the street he goes run stumbling with the lady after him waving the broom just as he hits the corner a police car turns down the street and the lights flash quick burst of siren before the cop car jumps the curb right in front of Ryan he runs right into the back end falls to the street cops step out of the car and they all say we better get the fuck out of here. . .

. . . if Mother and Father find out about this, the shit is going to I don't even want to think about what the shit is going to do but I have to forget about that, forget mother and father, I have got to hold it together here, hold it because there is no way these fuck-ups will, go the thoughts in Stephen's head as they sit around Bug's kitchen table very shaky Frances crying a bit everyone saying, what are we going to do what are we going to do we should go to the police station. Stephen tells them, we are on acid and we should not go to the police station that will only make it worse for Ryan and for us, he tells them that the police will just call his mom no one goes to jail for chips and that calms them down some, everyone talks about Ryan for another minute, how it must have been God getting Ryan back for the rock making those cops be there and Ryan could now be cursed by God for all eternity and Stephen tells them that God doesn't care about stain-glass windows and Henry says, maybe the Jewish God doesn't care but the Catholic God cares, he cares a lot, and then Frances says, how do you now it's a he? what? what? goes Henry. God, how do you know God is a he? Well for starters have you seen the pictures, he is always a dude in the books and the movies and the conversation continues on stupid to Stephen like that, when all of a sudden it is stopped by that front-door-opening sound, Bug's Mom home from work so quick so hide in Bug's room run run run . . .

. . . pulled out of the car and into the station where there are about to Ryan three hundred cops and one says something in fast French that he doesn't quite get so someone gives him a poke from behind so Ryan turns to tell him to come on lay off, the words not even out of his mouth when the world turns upside down the big desk cop has him by the hair pulling him wrong way round till he is staring at the ceiling cop yelling in his face and Ryan is yelling back why don't you arrest some real bank robbersheroindealerschildmolesters coupled with a feeble struggling punch and the very next second it is into a back room, sleeves rolled up and a phone book and the billy-clubs waving and Ryan so scared he starts to cry cry cry and they all relax laugh laugh laugh OK OK OK, come on little girl, and Ryan gets led down to a cell where they take away his shoelaces belt and clang clang go jail jail doors . . .

. . . to the bathroom for a piss and on the way back Henry passes the TV room and Bug's mom asks, what are you kids doing in there? Science project, he tells her and then stands in the door and looks at the TV with her but really at her who is stretched out on the couch her skirt riding up and he thinks swears she is wearing garters, stares at her legs hoping she'll move hoping that skirt will sneak up another inch hoping she will put her hand between her legs and slowly start to rub hoping she will open her blouse pinch thick nipples through lacy bra hoping she will ask him to come sit down come sit closer as she pulls the skirt and bends over the couch slowly waving her big beautiful stretched ass out in the air slides her hands between her legs running one finger along wet middle-aged frosted pussy lips and there is a voice her warm voice saying Henry . . . Henry? . . . are you alright? . . . Henry? . . . are you OK? . . . and Henry blink blink blinks back to Bug's mom looking at him funny, so real casual-like he says, oh yeah fine, just wondering what this show is, don't think I've ever seen it before, she looks at him even funnier then says, it's the news, Henry.

Just when Bug thinks it's done it starts up again and everyone says I don't know or maybe it never stops and it seems like they've been high for eight nine years when Bug looks at the clock and it is only 7:27 and we got to get out of here, so quick bye bye Mom, and they are wandering up one street and down the next up one then down while the sky burns black.

After they get home, Ryan tries to explain the whole thing, little bits of light still flashing in the corner of his eyes. Tells her sorry he'd been drinking a little beer so sorry so stupid. The police said you couldn't even stand when they brought you in, she says. And who are you going to believe, the cops or me? She looks at him, and maybe it's the drugs, and maybe it's something else, but Ryan can, for the briefest moment see through her eyes looking back at him, and of course doesn't believe either, not even for the briefest moment. His mom just says just go to bed, real tired-like. From his room Ryan listens to her walk around slow, turn off the lights, then close her door, and thinks it is all true I am the bad bad person.

Henry tries to get Frances to come over to his place, but no way she just wants to get home be alone in her room, where she calls Ryan's house, lets it ring, his mom answers, she hangs up. But there were no witnesses plus Ryan was wearing gloves when he threw the rock so there'll be no fingerprints on it they can dust that rock all they want but they won't get any prints off it. Good point Henry, and she gets off the phone. Then down on her knees at the edge of bed God, please, please take care of Ryan, he didn't mean it about the rock, and it was just a window anyway, so please make him be OK . . .

When is this going to end? wonders Bug. Lies in bed but can't sleep so starts to beat off and ends up thinking about Frances in her panties standing up there on that diving board. Wipes his cum on the old towel he keeps under the bed, then looks at the ceiling thinking crazy stuff till, thank god, he finally falls asleep.

When is this going to end? wonders Stephen. Lies in bed but can't sleep so starts to beat off and ends up thinking about Frances in her panties standing up there on that diving board. Wipes his cum on the old towel he keeps under the bed . . .

When is this going to end? wonders Ryan. Lies in bed but can't sleep so starts to beat off and ends up thinking about Frances in her panties standing up there on that . . .

When is this going to end? wonders Henry. Lies in bed but can't sleep so starts to beat off and end ups thinking about Frances in her panties standing up there on that diving board, about Bug's mom in her panties bent over the couch, about Frances and Bug's mom together in their panties kissing bent over a diving board. Wipe his cum on the old towel he keeps under the bed, then looks at the ceiling thinking crazy stuff till, thank god, he finally falls asleep.

When is this going to end? wonders Frances. Lies in bed but can't sleep so starts to beat off and ends up thinking about herself in panties standing up on there that diving board. The boys are all there naked and on their knees at the edge of the pool. She looks down at them. They look up at her. She tells them to start and they do. She is standing up there on that diving board and they are all looking at her all stroking and all their eyes are on her standing there. One by one they start shooting white jags onto the tile floor and all eyes still on her standing all still stroking her all for her for all for she is cuming cuming cum, then looks at the ceiling thinking crazy stuff till, thank god, she finally falls asleep.

PETERBOROUGH
Shithole

The show was supposed to be at a club but the club is not a club it is a brightly lit pool hall under a laundromat, which pretty much sums it up. After Tim and I go to a party at the local punker house, which the kids have dubbed Big White on account of it being big and white. We sit out on the porch with a blender. Listen to the whir of its tiny motor. Look at the streetlights that mark the front lawns and asphalt, silver pools that stretch from us to the end of the block. We drink the margaritas chased by the peach schnapps smoke all the reefer laugh with the kids for the rest of the night with the predictable results . . . Tim ends upstairs with a lady in her thirties and leather pants. I go down to the basement and share a stained mattress with a large-breasted girl whose father teaches at the university. We almost have sex, but are too drunk, so fall asleep with our pants around our ankles. Morning comes, my head splits in two. I sit on the porch with the girl, and she talks a lot about visiting me and how much fun that would be and what is my phone number and I say, Oh, I'll give it to you before I go, and she says, Don't forget, and then a few more people come and sit on the porch and we sit and sip coffee till Tim finally comes down looking like death barely thawed let alone warmed over, and I and say, We should go, we're really late, we better go. The girl looks at me, but I, of course, don't mention the number, just wave walk away like an asshole.

THE PUNK ROCK SHOW pt. 1

Hurry up, says Stephen. Yeah hurry the fuck up, says Henry. Just a second, Ryan answers as he takes a last look at himself in the mirror: one pair pants, black, straightened and too short; one pair postman shoes, black; socks, one yellow, one bright green; one blazer, tartan; one t-shirt, dirty white; one wrist band, studded. Then he pulls at his hair. It won't stay up on one side.

– Come on we're going to miss the show, says Stephen.

– OK, OK.

– You're worse than a girl, says Henry.

– Silence motherfuckers, Ryan tells them, I'm fixing my hair. He gives it one last pull, then turns and asks, Are you guys ready? Fuck off, says Henry. Come on, let's get out of here, Ryan adds. No really, finishes Henry, fuck off.

Ryan's mom is in the kitchen having her after work coffee and cigarette. Stephen and Henry wait in the hall while he goes in to give her a kiss. Bye Mom, he says.

– Don't be late. It's a school night.

– Don't worry, I won't.

– Here, let me give you some money, in case you need to take a cab. While she's gone he grabs a few smokes from her pack. They're not his brand – too light – but if you tear off the filters they're not half bad. She comes back with five dollars, which she gives him with a hug. Look at your hair Ryan, she says and tries to smooth it down. Aw c'mon mom, he tells her, you're wrecking it.

The three meet Bug and Frances at the Metro, then it's under the ground to the other side of town. Inside the club it's better than they ever could have imagined: girls in rubber, dog collars and chains; mounds of black eye-liner mixed with torn fish-net stockings; guys in leather motorcycle jackets and real brothel creepers from the King's Road; army boots, bondage pants, Dr. Martins; safety pins keeping it all together; there's even a girl with a stringy sweater, just like the Pistols wear. The kids group together by the side of the stage, smoking cigarettes and drinking the booze they've smuggled in, trying so very, very hard to look cool.

When the lights go off, the crowd rushes the stage, cramming down in front. We're going to see the Clash, the kids think, the fucking Clash! They can see dark shapes moving around on stage. The band is plugging in. Then one dark shape approaches the mic: *Mesdames et Messieurs, maintenant c'est mon plaisir de vous presentez . . . Lucien Francoeur*! Big white lights flash on. The music starts. At center stage is a balding French man with really long hair growing down the back and sides. He's wearing a leather vest, faded flared jeans, and snakeskin cowboy boots. The kids all think: He's a fucking hippy! And the rest of his band, they're fucking hippies too! It's an opening band and they are all fucking hippies! And we hate fucking hippies! And they are playing some shit French blues/rock song! This, think the kids, is un-fucking-believable!

The audience stands stunned, too dumbfounded to even move. Henry says, fuck this shit. He launches a huge brick of spit into the air. It passes through the white stage light, shimmering end over end, sailing alone through the air until it slaps onto the side of the lead singer's face. His eyes open wide with shock and he looks down at the five dumb drunk-kid faces who are calling him a fucking asshole, giving him the finger, telling him to get the fuck off of the stage. He takes a step in their direction and Henry launches another missile. It lands on the fringe of his leather vest. Ryan sends one and it catches him on the arm. He takes another step. All of a sudden there is a roar from the crowd, and a huge barrage of spit begins. There's a steady stream of it, a disgusting rainstorm showering down on the band. Absolutely fucking amazing, think the kids.

The lead singer is looking around, no idea what to do. Henry takes advantage and launches a half empty beer can, which clips him on the shoulder. He turns and there they are again, furious drunken children giving him the finger, telling him to fuck off back to Woodstock, fuck off back to Chicoutimi. He raises his mike stand and comes running toward the edge of the stage, swinging like he is off to the races. Ryan heaves the half empty bottle of cider, hoping to give him something else to aim for. The bottle goes flying through the air and hits the lead singer in the chest. He stumbles back, drops the stand. Henry and Ryan jump up and down in mighty celebration.

All of a sudden everything goes black. Ryan's blazer pulled over his head, and he's being dragged along very fast, bumping into many things. Then he's going down. He loses his footing and falls forward, but instead of hitting ground, he finds himself floating on through the air, then smashing into something head first and hard. Lights explode behind his eyes as he comes to rest in a crashing of metal and wood. Ryan uncovers his head, looks up. Two huge bouncers are standing in a doorway. One of them says something in quick French and then slams the doors shut. It's quiet in the alley. A lone streetlamp casts just enough light to see. Ryan is lying in a pile of garbage. Henry is right beside him, his mouth bleeding. Bastards, he says. Fuckers, Ryan agrees. They both jump up and start pounding on the doors. They bash till their hands are almost gone. Ryan is just about to give up hope, just about to light a smoke, when the door pops open, and there is Joe Strummer. Hair slicked back, white pants with motorcycle boots and a red shirt, cigarette hanging out of his mouth. Henry and Ryan can't form one single word. They just stand there staring. Well OK kids, says Joe, come on in then.

GUELPH

University of Guelph

Sound check. They are trying to play Like A Rolling Stone. Again. Tim fucks it up. Again. Phil stops strumming. Stupid hung-over dick he calls him. Then he turns to me, Bug, you're supposed to take care of him. That's your job. Anyone can carry a guitar, you just remember that motherfucker. Then unplugs his and walks off muttering what's the fucking use etc. Show is as to be expected. Back in the van Phil asks where are we going when I turn off into the mall parking lot. Tell him I need more cigarettes. Except for a couple of zitty kids in nylon uniforms and one bored cashier reading gossip mags the Food City is ours. Tim and I set off down the first aisle. By the time we get done Phil, Sara and Chuck are standing around in the parking lot, just like I planned, spread out, alone and weak, like sick wildebeests on the Serengeti. Tim and I get as close as we dare then break into a run, opening the egg cartons and firing from the hip. Bam bam bam. Phil is my main target, but everyone gets it. Cold-blooded killers on the road. I grab whip cream cans and move in for the finish. Eggs dripping everywhere. Phil is cursing. Chuck is laughing. Sara is begging: no Bug no Bug don't . . . please! But there is no mercy. Not in our business. It's kill or be killed. And I am a killer. Then bang an egg explodes on the back of my head, then another on my shoulder. I turn and Tim laughing hysterically pitches one more that hits me square in the chest. Chuck slips up from behind and grabs whipped cream out of my hand and it is in my hair down the side of my face. Sara has my bag. Out comes the syrup. Two bottles. Double-barreled. Sticky sweetness everywhere. I try to run but there are too many of them. They pin me in against the van. You can't trust anyone these days. Out comes the bag of flour. Everything goes white.

THE HOMECOMING

When his father picked him up he pretty much looked the way
Henry remembered: dark hair, wire-frame glasses, corduroys. It
was early and out on the apartment steps the air was still cool.

– Hello Dad, Henry said.

– Hello Henry, said his father.

Henry's mom was out there on the steps with them. A bird
sat in a tree making noises. The tree stood in the yard in front of
the apartment building. His mom's arms were folded across her
chest. Then she tucked a strand of hair behind her ear.

– This looks like a nice place, Cath, his father said.

– Well Paul, I'm glad you like it.

– So, how are things?

– Good.

– And work?

– Work's good.

– Your mother?

– Mother is fine, Paul.

That bird was still making noises. Henry's father looked at his
watch. Well, I guess we better be going, he said.

The green Volkswagen was familiar like the father, cracked
vinyl seats, the missing ashtray and the smell of dry straw that
rose from the carpeted floor. Driving along the highway the sky
was clear and the sun shone brightly on the fields and the trees.

– So, how *is* your mother? his father asked.

– Oh she's good, Henry told him.

A bit later they stopped for breakfast at a fast-food restaurant. After ordering Henry found a table and looked out the window. Across the highway sat a strip-bar and a hardware store. A house or two. That was the town. Henry was thinking himself, OK, now just where the fuck are we? when his father said, I really think you'll like it out here. The farm is great, and there are always lots of people around. In fact, we're having a party today. Your uncle Dennis is coming and he's bringing Gina. You haven't seen them in awhile have you?

– No, Henry agreed.

His father picked up his coffee and took a sip. Then he said, that'll be fun. And you'll finally get to meet Marcy.

– Marcy's going to be there?

– She is really looking forward to meeting you. I've told her all about you. I'm sure you two will get along.

– Uh huh, Henry said and kept chewing his hash browns. Pretty soon they were back on the highway. Can I play a tape? Sure, said his father. Henry put it in and pressed play . . . *He's in love with Rock and Roll He's in love with getting stoned He's in love with Janie Jones But he don't like his boring job NOOOOO. . .* Henry, what is this? his father asked. It's the Clash, they're from England, Henry told him. Oh really, he said and then he didn't say anything else. Henry turned it up a bit more, and looked out the window . . . *Big business it don't like you It don't like the things you do . . . Cos killers in America work seven days a week . . . From Genesis to Revelation The next generation will be . . . And everybody doing Just what they're told to And nobody wants to GO TO JAIL . . . No Elvis Beatles or the Rolling Stones in 1977. . .*

After parking the car by a barn his father started off along a path. Henry followed a few feet behind. On the left a field of corn sat soft and yellow in the summer sun. To the right the ground dipped away into a large grass lined bowl. At the centre of the bowl lay a pond. Down there people were gathered around the water's edge. As they walked on, Henry looked at the people. No way, he thought to himself, no *fucking* way. But getting nearer he saw that it was true. The people down there weren't wearing clothes; in fact, they were totally naked!

Henry and his father kept on until they were by the water. Henry stuck his hands in his pockets and looked at a tree. He looked at a rock. He looked at the pond. The sun was bright reflecting off the surface. He walked over to the edge and watched it jump from wave to wave. Then he heard his father call his name. Turning around the first thing he saw was his father naked, and his penis was hanging there in the sunshine and the fresh air. Henry hadn't seen him since the Christmas before last, and now, after less than a few hours, he was hanging out in the sunshine and fresh air. Henry kept his eyes on his father's face as he talked. His father was making introductions. People were waving and saying hello. Everywhere Henry turned it was the same thing, breasts, leg, ass, hair. Even his cousin Gina, fourteen years old, pulled off her shirt and out they came.

Henry waited until the hellos were done and then casually strolled over to a tree near the water. He took off his shirt and folded it neatly. Next he did the same with his shorts. For a moment he stood there in his underwear thinking about it.

Though he was nervous about dropping them, the idea of being the only one parading around in underwear somehow seemed worse. Making his decision, he hooked his thumbs under the elastic band and tugged them down. Then he picked up an air mattress that was lying nearby and carried it into the pond.

The sun was hot on his shoulders and back. He kicked his feet in the water. The air mattress had raised head and armrests, and a clear plastic window on the bottom. He looked down into the deep green. Some weeds. A little fish. Then he looked at the shore where the people were lying on blankets or swimming in the water. In particular, he looked at one woman with red hair. She was wading in the water near the shore. Her red hair was long and thick. She walked with her shoulders back and her large breasts pushed forward. He looked at her breasts. They swayed as she waded, and between her legs flashed a patch of autumn. Henry lay on the rocking air mattress, watching the woman on the shore wading and swaying, his hard-on growing and growing.

Henry's cousin left her blanket, walked out into the water, and began swimming towards him. What are you doing out here, she asked when she got near.

– Just floating, her told her as he shifted awkwardly on the air mattress, trying to arrange himself. She tread water beside him. Glancing through the plastic window he could see her legs.

– So, what's new? she asked.

– Oh, not too much, he answered, you know, school.

– Right, me too, she said. He snuck another look at her pinwheeling white thighs.

– I hate my school. It sucks, she said.

– Yeah, me too, Henry agreed, school totally sucks.

Then they were quiet for a bit. Pretending to rub the side of his face he took another look. At the top of the legs he could just make out her pussy. She reached a hand out of the water to brush some hair from her eyes, then grabbed a hold of the air mattress to rest. Her breasts rose to the surface, bobbing like soft icebergs. There was less than a foot between them and Henry's face.

– That's tiring, she said and then asked, have you ever done this before?

– What?

– Swum like this . . . naked.

– No, I usually go to the pool. You have to wear a suit.

– It's nice isn't? It feels so free. Don't you think?

– Yeah, free, he told her. He wanted to look at her legs again, but was worried she would notice, so he smiled instead. She smiled back and then she said she was tired again. She asked if she could lean on the mattress. Sure, he said. As they talked she leaned on the air mattress more and more, and so more and more of her body came out of the water, and into the sun and air, like a baby seal on ice. There was more and more of her to look at, so Henry looked at more and more, and they talked and laughed. After awhile she was pretty much on the mattress with him, and it was slowly sinking under their combined weight. They laughed about that as they slid around trying not to sink, and their bodies brushed against each other, and though this made him feel drunk – maybe even better than drunk, he thought, if there was such a feeling – Henry also had this hard-on that he had to be careful with, and so, when she said she was going back, he was sad, but also relieved. She slipped off the mattress and into the water. See you on land, she said and then started swimming back

– OK, see you, he said. He watched her go. Her ass broke the water as she kicked. He was pretty sure he could see her pussy flashing between the cheeks. When he didn't think he could see her anymore, he turned his attention to other things. He looked at the water; at a dragonfly skimming over its surface; at the edges of the sky. Then he looked at the shore and caught sight of red hair again. She was on the grass playing frisbee, running and jumping, just throwing it all over the place. As Henry watched her play he thought about the woman, and his cousin, and about the all other people in the world, and their nakedness, and all the things that could happen with all of that. Sex was like a bottle of warm Pepsi. It fizzed up and spilled inside his head, covering his brain, all sticky and gumming everything. The sun was hot and the water rocked the mattress.

His father yelled, Henry time to eat. Henry had been drifting in and out of sleep, and at the sound of his name he opened his eyes. He listened to his father call twice more before lifting his hand to wave, and then slowly he began to paddle in. When he kicked, he noticed that his hard-on was still there, maybe even worse now. It got in the way as he tried to organize the movement of his legs.

When he got near, Henry lifted his head and looked to the shore. There were still a few people there. He slowed his paddling, and tried waiting for a bit, counting how many Cups the

Montreal Canadiens had won, and in which years, all-time team leading scorers, and so on . . . but it was no help, the hard-on would not go. He rolled off the mattress and into the water. Lying just beneath the surface he let the air slip out of his mouth, and down into the cool dark he went. Happily, he felt his cock began to shrink.

At the shore he hauled the mattress out of the water then walked toward the small group where his father stood waiting. With him was a man Henry didn't know, and then behind them a face he had missed while pulling mattress from pond. Henry, this is Ted, said his father, and this is Marcy. Ted waved. With a big smile Marcy walked right up, her red hair flowing, and wrapped her arms around his shoulders hugging him tight. It's so nice to finally meet you, she said with her mouth at his ear. She held on rocking Henry back and forth. Her breasts were pressed against his chest. He could feel her nipples on his skin. They felt hard. He started to get nervous with all the rocking and pressing. And those nipples. Much worse, as she held him, he felt himself start to stiffen up again. Henry looked at his father from over her shoulder and he was smiling at him. Weakly, Henry smiled back.

The rocking and pressing continued. Henry felt himself swell all the way. He shut his eyes and prayed, hoping it would pass, but blood was pounding in his head, and behind his eyelids danced breasts and asses, lips and cheeks. The world melted away. All he could hear was the sound of breath pulling in and out. All he could smell was hair and skin. All he could feel was a rocking back and forth. Then his cock came to rest on something soft. Immediately the rocking stopped. But Henry did not. He pushed his hips forward, felt his cock jerk a few inches across warm skin. Once. Twice. That was all it took. Henry shook as his insides were tugged out through that small hole at the end of his cock; rattled as horses raced through pounding surf; rolled as a lonely train pulled away from the station. He sighed when there was nothing left, no shakes, or rattles, or rolls, and for the smallest second he was a pebble sinking gently to the green bottom . . . and then the world came rushing back: the sun on his face, his cum on her stomach, and somewhere just behind them a father.

KITCHNER/WATERLOO
University of Waterloo

Apparently there was some kind of booking mess-up at the University, because when we show up there is no show, but who really cares because we're going fishing. Well, some of us are. Phil's winsome attitude is not much improved by the cancellation and he once again storms off. Sara stays around the motel napping. Chuck, Tim and me head out in the van with Russ this young kid from some local band who was supposed to open. We come around the bend and there it is big beautiful water. Out in the boat we don't have much luck. A few perch, couple of bass. Mostly smoke pot (though not Chuck who is straight-edge as they come coffee and aspirin the strongest drugs he ever touches) and tell dumb tour stories: this band that band this girl that girl this town that town this time I got wasted and fell out of a window that time I got wasted and fell out of a window. Then Russ starts asking us about Making It. He really wants his band to Make It, and wants to know if we have any advice about Making It. That, I say, is something we are totally unfamiliar with. Tim advises, brush and floss after each meal, and leaves it at that. But Chuck starts in telling the kid about how it used to be bands didn't worry about Making It, they worried about Selling Out. How there used to be a time when bands didn't have publicists and five-year plans, a time when everyone hated videos and radio and believed strange old stuff like corporate music sucks. Russ just sits there looking at Chuck like he's wearing a shit beard. Kids these days, but I guess you have to cut them some slack. Brought up post-Madonna. Suckled at Ronald McDonald's teat.

They don't know anything else. They Just Do It, and so much better designed to survive nowadays than us. On the bright side, I get a bite, three pound bass on the end of the line, biggest fish of the day! On the way back the van winds down those country roads.

ALL THE YOUNG DRUNKS

They loaf along Sherbrooke Street, looking at themselves in the store windows. Stephen decked out in torn peg-legged jeans and white high-cut Chuck Taylors, ratty v-neck sweater, topped with a head of greasy spikes. Ryan sporting his favourite red windbreaker, much like J. Dean's in *Rebel Without A Cause*, straightened old-man black pants, army boots, and fresh pumpkin lid. They jump, make faces, agree they are very cool, then stop for Joe Louies and Cokes. Sitting outside the Mac's Milk the boys watch the traffic. When this gets dull, Ryan steps into the alley for a piss. Ten seconds go by and all of a sudden he is shouting his friend's name. Stephen skids round the corner, only to find Ryan standing in front of a wall of beer cases. There must be a hundred. All the beer you could ever want, whispers Ryan, all ours for the taking. He is staring at them like it's the second coming of something or other. Stephen watches as Ryan opens a case, then another, and another, and another, then looks up with tears in his eyes, but they are not tears of joy, oh no, they are tears of sorrow, because the bottles in the cases are empty. Further inspection proves they are all empty, every bottle in every case, empty. They light cigarettes to commiserate the near, rare brush with blessed fortune. Ryan starts flipping bottles into the air, and Stephen is listening to the sound of breaking glass, when it comes to him: the big picture . . . the concept . . . the way! They carry cases to every other store in the neighbourhood, at ten cents a bottle, two dollars and forty

51

cents a case, one hundred and thirty seven dollars plus change by the time they are done.

This calls for a celebration, says Ryan, as he spies the *Festivale du Homard* sign over the restaurant door and there is no reasoning with him. They start with beer and tequila and then come the lobsters, three each, and plates of french fries. Stephen looks up from his half-done to see Ryan wrestling, still trying to crack the bright red shell. Have you had lobster before? No, not really. Stephen shows him how to crack it open, and then listens to him go on, this is fantastic, this is fucking delicious, this is absolutely my new favourite fucking food. Stephen looks up again two minutes later, and in his enthusiasm Ryan is trying to eat the head and antennae. Don't do that, Stephen tells him. Ryan flips it over his shoulder like Friar Tuck in *Rocket Robin Hood* and says, more beer!

The doorman takes one look at them and shakes his head. I'm nineteen and he's twenty, Ryan nods toward Stephen, who is standing right behind him, five foot three, ninety seven pounds, glasses, and dressed, as far as the doorman is concerned, like a total fag. We got tons of money, big tips, says Ryan as he pulls his wad out, but it quickly becomes apparent that fat disco Italian guys who work the door at strip bars are not impressed by drunk fifteen year olds with funny hair and a fistful of twenties. He shifts off his stool with menace, suggesting they get the fuck out and don't ever come back. They are following his advice when the door swings open and through it they can see into the dark where red and green lights wink, and a woman with the biggest set of real live fully naked fake tits either of them have ever seen comes shaking by, their stares catch her eye, and as the door swings back shut she laughs, smiles and waves. Oh my god, they tell each other, those tits, did you see those tits, those tits, did you see, as they tramp down Mountain Street on the way to Blues, a floundering discotheque that has hit such sub-marine financial depths that they've taken to letting in any drug addict, gay skinhead, new wave mom, drag queen, punk rocker, or dumb drunk kid who has the two dollar cover.

The beer bottle sails by Ryan's head and hits the side of a red Camaro. They both turn to see jocks hanging out a sports bar window. Big jocks, grade eleven at least, thinks Stephen, maybe even college age, with beady eyes bugging out of red faces, baseball hats screwed on tight, foam dripping from chapped lips, big muscles squeezing for a place at the window to scream faggots fucking cocksucking fucking faggots faggots fucking. Aww go screw yourselves, says Ryan and flips them the bird. The blustering red faces immediately disappear from the window. The boys start running. Don't look back till they hit the corner. The jocks are close on their heels. Ryan sprints into the traffic, Stephen right behind, and they dodge cars for half a block, then down the alley between Mountain and Crescent, up a fire escape to the roof of a garage, lie low, peek over the edge. Seconds later the jocks come racing around the corner. They slow down, sluggishly figuring their prey couldn't have made it all the way to the end of the alley, their little brains just starting to tell them to look for hiding places, when someone else comes huffing around the corner. Step into the light, and it is the doorman from the strip bar saying, which one of you little fucks threw a bottle at my car? The jock leader says fuck you. Fuck me? Fuck me? Fuck me? Fuck me? the fat doorman keeps repeating as he walks up to the jock and kicks him right in the balls. Fuck me? Fuck me? Fuck me? The eternal question punctuates his kicks to the jock who lies on the concrete, while jock friends just stand and watch, as do Ryan and Stephen, from ringside seats, peaking their heads over, then ducking down and exchanging looks of pure glee.

We have to get to Las Vegas, says Ryan, because we will never be this lucky again in our entire lives! This is as good as it ever gets! The bartender brings two cold Heinekens, two cold vodkas, and down they go, and there at the end of the bar are two girls, and Ryan reasons when the world is your oyster . . . their names are Marie-Claire and Yvette, and they are very punk. Marie-Claire has big black hair hanging over a cute little red tartan mini, com-bat boots, ripped nylons, red, white and blue sweat band, t-shirt with the sleeves rolled up, thick red lips and rivers of black black massacre eyes. Ryan doesn't notice Yvette as much, but she is taller, tight black jeans, bullet belt, and bleached hair, he thinks. He buys Marie-Claire a beer, and they chat about he doesn't really know what because her English isn't very good, and he can't speak much French. The DJ puts on *Wild Youth*, Marie-Claire jumps up saying, this is my favourite song. She grabs his hand, and though Ryan thinks Gen X are more or less crap, he also thinks who really cares about that now. Out on the floor, mohawks and bracelets bash around, Ryan has another sip of beer, trips over a stool, then Marie-Claire takes his hand and pulls him into the girls washroom, where the three girls fixing their hair make-up don't take much notice as they make their way to a stall. Marie-Claire closes the door behind them and starts rummaging through her bag. Out comes a little bit of tinfoil, she looks up and says, do you want some speed? They snort it off the back of the toilet, race to the bar for more Heinekens and more vodka, then onto the floor for more dancing with the big sweaty whirl-wind of bodies that careens across the floor, bouncing off the walls, Ryan's arms around Marie-Claire, and here we go here we go up here we go down go up and down up and down and here we go . . .

Yvette seems nice enough, laughing along with Stephen's jokes, asking how old he is, asking where he learned to speak French, asking if he has a girlfriend, so it seems to be going well, though she is sort of tall, and he is sort of short, so his head must always tilt up or be talking to her breasts, which is sort of awkward, though not awful. Stephen buys another round, and from the bar can see Ryan and Marie-Claire going up and down. He walks back to Yvette, but she is now talking to a big ugly skinhead. Behind him another bald head eyes Stephen suspiciously. He catches Marie-Claire's name, and then where the fuck is she, as the uglier one peers out onto the dance floor. Stephen looks back as well, but happily Marie-Claire and Ryan are now nowhere to be seen. Less happily, the two skinheads are now giving Stephen the once over taking in the dark hair, glasses, nose, and, thinks Stephen, I might as well have JEW written in marker across my forehead. The uglier one snatches Yvette's fresh beer from his hand, drinks it down, then leans right into Stephen and lets out a massive ripping belch, much like the gorillas in comics, yelling full in your face, blowing the hair back. Stephen bumps up against a wall, waits to have to his arms plucked off, but Yvette is there, talking something in an ear, and the bald head looks confused for a moment, then turns and stumbles off into the club's darkness. Yvette says in English coated thick and sexy with French, don't worry about him, he's an asshole. Then she puts her arm around Stephen's shoulder, gives a squeeze, and pulling his face wonderfully close to her left breast says, I like your hair, it's cute. Could Ryan actually be right, wonders Stephen, could this actually be the luckiest night of their lives?

Ryan follows her back to the bathroom, past three different girls, into the same stall. He closes the door, priming his nose for another stinging jolt, when Marie-Claire bangs up against him, her tongue rushing into his mouth, her hands into his jeans. Seconds later her nylons are down and he is doing his best to get his cock up inside her. She grabs hold and puts it against her lips, but they can barely get the head in. Ryan feels he is trying to squeeze into a tight, sandy rabbit hole. Is everything all right? he asks. It's just the speed, she whispers, don't worry baby, as she spits on her hand, slathers it over his cock, and soon enough Ryan is half in and her pussy starts to open up, heat up, pull him up, till he's sunk all the way, hips touch hips. Marie-Claire gasps and bites his shoulder, as his hands hurry up her shirt, little nipples brightening like stars, down below things starting slowly at first out then in then faster fast fastest full on fucking into each other, and the stall is shaking, and mysterious words pouring lovely into Ryan's ear.

Yvette comes back rolling her eyes. So? asks Stephen. They are fucking, she says, in the bathroom, they are fucking, and it is very noisy. She laughs and sits down beside him, her thigh pressed close up against his, and doesn't say anything else, but her words seem to hang there, like an indication, maybe even an invitation. Yvette is smiling. She is looking at him. He is looking at her. Stephen's heart is racing. He is about to say something like . . . something like . . . something . . . like . . . some . . . thing . . . like . . . do you . . . want . . . to . . . have another beer? Sure, she smiles. Stephen shakes his head on the way to the bar. When I get fucking back, he fucking promises himself, I will be accepting that fucking invite.

. . . *Oui* . . . *Oui* . . . *Oui* . . . Marie-Claire's left foot on the toilet bowl, right one against the door, with Ryan in the middle just trying to hold on, to not fall over backward, to do his best, when here comes the cumming, white lights behind his eyes, roman candles firing out and then pulling back, keep going, going, please just a few more, and there she goes too . . . *Oui Oui Oui Oui oh Oui* . . . shaking, making her breath come in tiny gasps, his t-shirt curled up in her little fists, lips tugging at his ear. Then out into the club again, the music washing over them, as they find Yvette, find their cigarettes, find drinks, find Stephen coming back from the bar with two beers and a funny fucking look on his face.

Stephen waits for the chance to talk to Yvette, to somehow bring them back to the days of thigh to thigh, of invitations in the nightclub air, but Ryan and Marie-Claire keep talking talking talking and then Marie-Claire asks Yvette if she has any more speed, and after a bit more talk it comes out that there is no more speed left, and this touches off another debate that goes on in French for awhile, till Ryan looks at Stephen and asks, what's the big problem. Drug problems, he tells him, the problem is that there are no more drugs. Ryan pulls out forty dollars says, well, that's no problem. Marie-Claire takes the money, and they stand up and put on their coats. We'll be back in half an hour. There is a weird moment of them looking at each other, and then she says, I'll be back. I know you will, says Ryan. She leans down and kisses him good-bye. Yvette winks Stephen a see you soon.

The dance floor is flooded as the night ends. Stephen curled up on the corner of the couch asleep. Ryan is days from sleeping and watches bodies move and bump through the red blue black, and there is still no sight of Marie-Claire or her friend. Ryan wonders if he should feel bad, getting beat for the forty and left to wait, but doesn't because the night is still perfect and still spilling from the basement of his soul to the stars in the sky. He wants it to stay like this forever, to be tingling alive and hurtling head on into the new busted wide open, to be going forward, to be beginning, but the house lights pop up to say it's over, and the people blink around, looking for their jackets, looking for their friends, looking for their one last anything, and then it's the final song to usher them out onto the three a.m. city streets, a bit of guitar and fuck me Ryan thinks they would have to play this . . . *the Greyhounds rocking out tonight to maximum rock-a-billy . . . when two punks chose to risk the subway for a tube to Piccadilly . . . whose efforts serve as gangster glory . . . another dumb casualty . . .* dun dun ta dun . . . *having fun . . .* dun dun ta dun . . . *the sound of six hidden late night flicks . . . oh, kiss me . . . deadly . . . toonniiigghhhhtttttttttttt* . . . yeah, sure, Gen X might be pretty much crap, but you have to admit that sometimes they do almost get it just right.

What the motherfuck!? . . . what the where!? . . . lights on, asks Stephen then looks up at his friend . . . Ryan? Where are we? The club? Still? What? What time is it? Three-thirty? Three-fucking-thirty? Ryan my folks are going to fucking kill me. Come on, come on, let's go, let's get the fuck out of here. I can't believe you, I can't fucking believe you let me do that. Fuck. Motherfuck fuck fuck. . . fuck!

LONDON
Call The Office

London. Ontario. Home to frat boys, sorority girls and insurance sales-
men. I recommend it to cocksuckers and everyone I hate. The band
plays a bit better tonight. Mood seems a bit better. After Tim and I
hang around the club shooting beer drinking pool. Start talking with
two college girls, then play partners. Tim's partner is Alison. Mine is
Gidget. They are real college girls and look it: Alison blonde and smi-
ley; Gidget very pretty with serious long black hair; small animals on
their shirts, tretorns on their feet. Closing time we shuffle around for a
bit before it's agreed we'll go back to their place. Tim and Alison take
her car, but apparently it's not far, and Gidget wants some fresh air, so
off we go. Smoke a joint on the way, she takes a puff or two and
coughs, but we don't talk much, each of us thinking our thoughts. The
town keeps quiet too. Big houses and basketball hoops nailed to
garages. Football games and high school dances. Raking leaves and
Sunday dinners. Gidget breaks the St. Elmo's Fire moment with, I bet
you think I'm just some nice college girl. You seem nice, I tell her. She
stops, is that what you think, that I'm nice and boring? She looks
angry, and that starts to annoy for obvious Richie Rich reasons, so I
tell her she is nice. Very nice. In fact, I tell her, you are the probably
nicest fucking person I have ever met in my entire fucking life. Little
tears start in her eyes, and I start to feel bad, cause it can be hard, even
for real college girls. Sorry, I say. Oh fuck sorry. Then she is down on
her knees, tugging at my jeans. How nice is this? she asks, then
doesn't ask again, because she has my cock in her mouth. Now wait

a second, but she has really started, and I generally don't stop this type of thing, so I lean back against the car behind me, a Volvo station wagon. When she comes up we're both pretty committed to fucking. She bends over the hood of the Volvo, I slide in for hard fast strokes, and she pushes back into each one. Just about to go off, something catches my eye. A middle-aged woman is watching from the doorway of the closest house. Our eyes lock. We're practically on her lawn. Probably her Volvo. Gidget now cumming very hard gives us one last mighty shake and I shoot my load looking into the eyes of a housewife. London Ontario, fantastic fucking town.

THE SUFFERINGS OF JUDAS

Look at this, called Stephen, come on out here and just look at this. Ryan slid out of bed and into the sunshine. Stephen was standing on the porch of the boathouse in his underwear. Below them the lake stretched calm and quiet except for . . . can you believe this shit, pointed Stephen. In the middle of the bay two fishermen were sitting in a big speedboat. Motherfuckers, said Stephen, fishing in my goddamn bay . . . big . . . fat . . . mother-fuckers, he rapped his knuckles on the railing in time.

The boys balanced on the edge for a second, jumped out into the air, yelling FUUCCCKKKKK YOOUUUUU FUUCCKKKKK-EERRRRSSSS, then splashed into the lake. Ryan came up first and a moment later Stephen broke the surface snorting water. They paddled around on their backs watching the fishermen haul up anchor, waving good bye as they pulled out of the bay: so long, pricks! Then they headed up to the cookhouse for breakfast.

Mrs. Sauermann had laid out everything for them on the table, full glasses of orange juice in front of their plates, the Cheerios box, slices of bread waiting in the toaster. Stephen went into the kitchen and started cooking bacon and eggs. He turned on the radio and whistled along to the classic rock sta-tion. Ryan poured a cup of coffee and sat at the dining table. There was a note propped against the sugar bowl explaining that the Sauermanns had gone into town for the day. Stephen came in with two plates. Here you go, city boy, he said. For a skinny kid who wore glasses, thought Ryan, he sure turned pretty Grizzly Adams once he hit the trees, fresh air and sunshine.

After breakfast they sat on the cookhouse porch and got high. In the yard stood two large oaks with an old wooden swing hanging between them. Past the trees was the big house where Stephen's parents slept. The boys handed the joint back and forth as the sun stretched on the grass. The rest of the morning was spent lazing down on the dock. They swam and read old magazines. Flies drifted about, fat and lazy in the heat. Out on the water a few boats passed by. The boys smoked more pot. Swam some. Read another magazine.

Before long it was time to eat again. Ryan made the sandwiches, tomatoes with purple onions and cheddar cheese, while Stephen mixed a jug of lemonade. They carried the food into the dining room. It was cooler in there, the curtains hung over the windows keeping the sun at bay. Ryan took a bite of his sandwich. The taste of onion filled his mouth, ran up his nose, and started his eyes watering little tears. He blinked and looked around the room. On the far wall was a picture of Stephen's father, Dr. Sauermann. The picture was tucked in the corner of a mirror. Above the mirror hung a stuffed fish. Sometimes Stephen complained about his father, that he was cold and distant and only cared about the old ladies who were his patients, but he didn't seem that bad to Ryan. In fact, Stephen's parents seemed pretty great. So Ryan assumed that Stephen, being from a regular Mother-and-Father family, just didn't really understand about life, working moms, disappearing dads, and all the other wonderful things that could happen.

In the picture Dr. Sauermann was carrying a load of fire-wood. His hat had been knocked forward so he could not see. There was a big smile on his face, and you could tell it was a funny moment, and Ryan thought about how they did not go in for pictures much at his house; though that, he had to admit, was mostly because they didn't have a camera. After the divorce his father had kept it, and his mom never got around to buying a new one. Ryan took another bite of his sandwich. Back came the little tears.

After lunch they napped in the upstairs of the boathouse. The kind of lazy half-sleep you have in the early afternoon when it is warm outside and there is nothing to do. Upon waking, Stephen announced it was time to fish. Downstairs, among the boats, oars and coils of rope, they began fixing up a pair of rods. Stephen told Ryan how to tie the leader and where to clamp the weights to the line. Make sure you use a big hook or you'll be pulling sunfish off the thing all day long, he told him. OK, Ryan said and pried one off the workbench that seemed large enough.

They grabbed the tackle box, a styrofoam container of worms, a few beers, and got into the smaller boat. Out on the lake the wind was blowing and the water choppy. When they reached the next island Stephen guided them into a sheltered lit-tle bay. He cut the motor and the boat slid silently along. On his command, Ryan heaved the anchor into the water and they came to a halt. Stephen moved to the middle of the boat. The boys sat there threading worms onto hooks, with the boat rock-ing gently underneath them.

When the rods were set Stephen said, OK, here's what you do. Pull the guard back till it clicks. Hold the line, with your finger, here. Put the rod over your shoulder, and then snap it forward, like this. He cracked the rod. The line swam out and then fell down into the lake. All you have to remember is not to start reeling until your line is down and in the water, because if you don't, it will stop feeding, OK?

OK, OK, said Ryan, and he watched as Stephen, perched on the Mercury with his feet resting on the edge of the boat, began casting easily into the dark green water near the shore; and he thought more about the picture of Stephen's father, and he felt the thing that was always missing in his life, in him, and maybe it was a dad, and maybe it wasn't; and he felt the thing that was in his life that shouldn't be there, the thing he forgot about when it wasn't happening, and when it was; but mostly he felt angry, he felt so very angry; and he spent the next little while thrashing around up front, jamming the reel, killing a lot of worms; and the sun sank a bit lower, and the shadows from the trees stretched out across the lake.

Ryan began to cast successfully, ten feet, fifteen, twenty. The first thing he caught was a small sunfish, the hook stuck firmly under his jaw. Ryan held him dangling on the line not knowing what to do. Hold the line in your left hand, said Stephen, run the other hand over his body, smoothing down those spines. Then grab him and hold him tight. Following the instructions carefully, Ryan began sliding his hand down the fish. It felt like a cold, slippery muscle. Suddenly the fish flipped and pushed one of the spikes into his palm. Jesus Christ, he said and let go to examine the wound. A small ball of blood was forming on his skin.

– Hurry up, said Stephen, you're going to kill it.

Ryan looked at the fish. He started to run his hand down toward the body again. As soon as Ryan touched his head the fish started to thrash about. You fucking fish, he yelled, I'm trying to save your cocksucking life . . . so please, please, stop fucking with me. The fish remained at the end of the line. Ryan held him up at eye level to yell. Beyond the fish he could see Stephen shaking his head.

Ryan tried again, and this time got his hand around the fish's body and held on tight. Grabbing the hook he twisted it away from the open mouth. To his surprise, the hook slid out easily, and Ryan was suddenly holding the freed fish in his hand. He tossed it over the side. For a moment the fish rested just under the surface then swam down deep. There you go, said Stephen with a big smile in his face, that wasn't so tough, was it?

– Oh yeah, Ryan told him, piece of cake.

It was a bit later that it happened. They had just smoked more pot and Ryan was sitting at the front of the boat staring into the water . . . when from the back of the boat he heard a loud whine. He turned to see Stephen's reel spinning like a roulette wheel. His eyes were wide. Get the net, he said quietly. Scrambling over the seat to pick it up, Ryan started the boat rocking. Stephen motioned with his hand to be careful. Ryan sat down and laid the net across his knees. They both watched the line disappearing into the water. Round and round went the reel. After awhile it began to slow and then stopped. Stephen took the handle between his fingers and slowly began to wind it in. There was no resistance. Patiently he turned the reel.

The first sign of a fight came as a gentle tug pulling the rod toward the water. Stephen continued reeling at the same pace. Then the rod jerked suddenly. Stephen held on but the line started to unwind on the drag, traveling back into the dark green. Stephen waited calmly for it to let up then began reeling in again. This went on, back and forth, but each time the fish ended up that much closer to the boat. Ryan sat by holding the net tightly.

The first time it jumped was a shock. There was a sharp pull on the line, then it went slack. Ryan stared intently at the point where it disappeared into the water. A second later the fish broke the surface near the shore. Ryan turned his head, but all he caught was the fat sound of it hitting the water.

– Did you see that . . . DID YOU FUCKING SEE THAT? called Stephen his eyes saucer large fastened on the rippling circles, that is a big fish Ryan, that is a very big motherfucking fish. When the fish got close things really livened up. It began to dive deep under the boat. Stephen was on his feet, jumping from one seat to the next, the rod out in front of him, trying to keep up, all the while reeling and cursing. This went on for a while, Stephen jumping and yelling, the boat rocking, and Ryan trying to keep out of the way. In the end, Stephen was able to bring him close, a long piece of green silver being gently pulled up along side the boat, attached by a thin nylon line, with the tail moving slowly, like a pet.

– Jesus fucking Christ, said Stephen staring at the fish. He took a moment to collect himself. OK Ryan my boy, here is what we are going to do, he said quietly, I am going to start lifting him, you get the net under him, and we are going get him in the boat.

– Right, said Ryan. He slipped the net into the water behind the fish. Stephen stood up front with the rod in his hands. The net passed over his tail.

– Easy Ryan, easy, said Stephen. Half the fish was in the net. OK, here we go. He lifted the rod, pulling the head toward the surface. Ryan swung the net underneath. The head broke the water's skin. Slowly the fish slipped out of the lake.

– Look at him. Oh my god Ryan, LOOK AT HIM! The fish was in the net and Ryan was kneeling, trying to get him up and over the lip of the boat. Stephen was standing with the rod held above his head. The sun shone from behind him. His smile was wide. A sudden gust caught his hair, blowing it back, and his flannel shirt snapped in the wind. At that moment the fish flipped inside the net. Its head shot up over the top, and before Ryan knew it, the fish's body was balancing on the rim. Ryan tried to move the net underneath him, but lost his balance on the slick wood seat and landed at the bottom of the boat. The net fell away from under the fish and into the boat where it became tangled in his feet. Looking up he saw Stephen with the rod lifted high and the fish dangling at the end of the line. It stayed that way for a second, Stephen and the fish against the sky, then the line snapped, and the fish fell back into the lake.

Dinner was pretty quiet. The Sauermanns had not returned from town. Stephen barbecued chicken, while Ryan fixed a salad. They laid it out on the dining room table and started eating. After a while Ryan asked, you want a beer. Sure, answered Stephen. A bit later he asked if he wanted another. That was all they talked about. After dinner they went to the big house to watch television. Stephen sat with his arms crossed and stared hard at the set. Ryan pretended he was watching too, but really he was replaying the moment when he let himself slip, and let the net drop, and let the fish fall back into the lake, and he was happy. At the end of the show Ryan said, OK, that's enough for me. OK, said Stephen and kept watching. Don't worry, you'll catch a bigger one tomorrow, Ryan added. Stephen couldn't even look up from the TV. Walking down the steps to the boat-house Ryan started to whistle.

He sat on the boathouse porch and smoked. He looked the lake. He looked the stars. And he continued to replay his moment of sweet, rare victory in this world of haves and have-nots. When that grew tired, he went back in, turned out the lights and slipped under cool sheets. A bit later Stephen came down. Ryan was almost asleep. He listened to Stephen's steps on the stairs, watched his dark outline cross the floor. Stephen sat down on the edge of the far bed. You awake? Sort of, Ryan told him. Stephen sat there for what seemed like a long time then said, no one ever caught a fish that big . . . not me . . . not my brother . . . not even my father . . . no one. And it sounded like he was crying. Then he lay down, and, after awhile, was snoring. The moon came up and filled the room with silver, while Ryan lay in bed and felt that he had done it all wrong, once again, and so he couldn't sleep, so eventually he tried praying to anyone, or anything, to please please please let him be someone else, some-one good, who did right things, please, and the waves washed against the dock like little wooden hardships sailing from broken harbours.

ST. CATHERINE'S
The Hideaway

When a bit hung over I need trucker food. Hamburger steak, mashed potatoes with peas and gravy, pie and five six cups of coffee. There is a diner somewhere near here I remember from last time. Step out into St. Catherine's. Ladies in stretch pants at the laundromat. Men with graying hair greased back in the tavern. Younger girls in metal t-shirts. Older dudes in firebirds. You wouldn't want it to happen to you, wouldn't want to be born out here, but you can almost understand what Bruce Springsteen was going on about. I find the diner, slide into a booth. Wait for the coffee. Gidget and Alison show up at sound check. It's a surprise, but not all bad. I take Gidget back to the motel before the show, but both of us are pretty tired, and maybe wanting to slow it down some, so we talk instead, about life parents friends when we were young and so on and so I find myself telling her about this little book we used to read in the first grade called l'histoire de le petit phoque, which in English means story of the Little Baby Seal, but in French the word phoque sounds exactly the same as the English fuck, and how we just couldn't believe that, me and my little friends Henry, Ryan, Stephen, Frances, sitting in class reading the story of the little fuck, how it blew our little minds, and how we though French people were just balls out crazy cause if you would call a baby seal fuck well you'd probably do anything, and we laugh about that, then fall asleep till it's time. The band plays a bit better, but nothing to write home about. Towards the end Phil's mic starts feeding back. I can see the charge jumping from the metal to his mouth. I'm yelling at the sound-

man, telling him to get his shit together or we are out of here. But the kids are digging it, and Phil is up there trying his best. Say what you like about him, at least the guy cares about what he does. Just then this one shock leaps from the mic, and I can see it Shazam to his face, and it knocks him back into his amp, and me and the soundman get into what you might call a fistfight, and the show sort of winds down. After Tim and Alison plan to bring it on, but Gidget and I are still kind of worn out. Back at the motel I can tell she still feels a bit weird about the other night, the Volvo and whatnot, so we lie in bed talking some more, then have real regular sex, and it's pretty good too.

ARE YOU THERE GOD, IT'S ME, FRANCES

Frances McCormick and her mother go by the Benny Farm, and Frances thinks bunch of red brick apartments, pretty as hospitals, originally set up for war veterans and their families, now home to mostly anyone without much, including the Benny Hill Gang. The Farm has a small park with a hill. That's where the Gang's name comes from. Some people will laugh when they hear it, because of that English comedian who hits the little old man chases girls with big tits around gardens. But the Benny Hill Gang aren't comedians. Not intentionally at least. They're skin-heads. You hear stories about them, machetes and big fights on football fields behind high-schools. I don't know about that, but last fall one of them punched Henry at a party. Right in the kitchen. Henry walked in, said something stupid, for a change, and this bald kid punched him. Right in the face. Then there were about twenty bald guys hitting everything in sight. Then it all moved out onto the lawn. Ryan, Bug and Stephen got beat up, and then Henry got beat up again. I can laugh about it now, but at the time I was scared and crying. It often happens that way. Not that I'm scared and crying. That the boys get beat up. For boys with such big mouths, they sure aren't very good at fighting. Anyway, that all really happened because Henry took his dog Sam for a walk by the Benny Farm park. The Gang was hanging on the swings. They asked Henry if he had any ciga-rettes. No, said Henry. Any money. He said he didn't. So they took the dog. Said they were holding Sam for ransom. Back at home Henry's Mom said, Ten dollars? For the dog? So she phoned her brother Terry who lives at the Belvedere Motel, near the Rose Bowl, down on the St. Jacques strip. You never know just exactly what he does for a living, but you have an idea: he wears white shoes and spends all his time at places like Nittolo's bar & grill. When the Gang saw him pull up in his El Dorado, and those big white shoes stepped out onto the sidewalk, they thought better and handed Sam back. Just then the bus stops at the corner of Madison, in front of the Mac's Milk where we often smoke cigarettes. A few more passengers squeeze on. The bus is full of people going downtown. Kids heading to the movies and the arcades, Christmas shoppers, and a few, like Mom and me, off to church. She let me go to public school instead of the Sacred Heart so Saturday it is Notre Dame Cathedral from three to five. Then St. Kevin's on Sunday ten thirty till noon. Every week. Like that. Though today I don't feel much like going to church. Not after last night. But don't think about all that. Not now. So I do what we do when we don't want to think: look out a window. We roll by Grand Avenue. My good friend Denise lives on the corner, over a bank. Next block is Hampton, and the Lav-O-Rama. Beside that is Old Jim's secondhand book and record store. Old Jim is fat as well as old and can hardly move. I can't see him from the bus but bet he is sitting behind the counter, smoking a cigar and watching game shows, while his five hundred cats roam the stacks of albums, weave by piles of books, spring from heap of junk to mountain of stuff. We spend days rooting that shop. Once Ryan found the first Velvets' album, the one with the banana sticker you can peel off. Old Jim sold it to him for one dollar. Still had the sticker on it! One dollar! But mostly you can only find the regular old stuff, and since most regular old stuff sucks, you really have to look hard. So far the old stuff we like includes: early Who, early Stones, Neil Young, T Rex, Mott the Hopple, Chuck Berry, Johnny Cash, Elvis, early Bob Dylan. But no Genesis, Pink Floyd, Yes, or any of that. That stuff is strictly for hippies. And we hate hippies. Though he doesn't seem to care much about music, Old Jim has some very strong thoughts on books, about what is good (Henry Miller, William Burroughs, Jack Kerouac, and the three mighty Hs . . . Hemingway, Hammett, Hamsun . . . though it is Mr. Charles Bukowski who holds the very special place in his heart), about what is bad (everything else). Personally, I prefer the ladies, Virginia Wolfe, Emily Dickinson, S. E. Hinton, and so on like that. Ryan is also a big reader, especially George Orwell, and this other British fellow Allan Sillitoe. We swap, go for coffee, talking about parts we liked, what it was about, and so on; but when everyone else is around Ryan acts like the only thing he ever reads is the side of the cereal box; like J.J. Kellogs is his favourite author. Henry is not much of a reader, except for the Gazette sport page and occasional Penthouse Forum. Sometimes I wonder how I ended up with him, since I have much more in common with Ryan, but then that's probably why. It's funny that I'm thinking of Ryan, because just now we go by the building where he lives with his mom. It's this big old brown apartment on the corner of Old Orchard. On the side someone has spray-painted: SHOULDN'T EVERYTHING BE BROWN? And that is sort of funny too. My mom opens her purse and starts searching for something. I keep my eyes pointed out the window watching my neighbourhood roll by: Notre Dame du Grace, which is French for Our Lady of

Grace. Coming up on our left is Cosmos restaurant, the best breakfast in the city. There's Mom's Caribbean Kitchen. Then NDG Park. Big grey trees line the sidewalk. Big mountains of snow covering last summer's grass. Winters here are so bad that sometimes people die and only get found in the spring when the drifts melt. It happened two years ago, to some poor lady from the out-patient clinic at the Queen Elizabeth. Across the street is the Cinema V where we see old movies, foreign ones, even the art films. We practically live there. Last week we went to see this one *The Passenger*, because of Jack Nicholson, but we couldn't understand it. He's just walking around not doing anything. Though we were really high, and maybe it's not that kind of movie. It's like this other time, Ryan and Henry went to something called *SALO: A Hundred And Twenty Days of Sodom*, when they were really wasted. They thought it was a sex movie. About ass sex. Something Henry is interested in. Very interested. But anyway, it was really about these Italian rich people who captured these kids in this castle and basically tortured them. Made them crawl around naked, eat shit, fucked every hole in their bodies. Henry said all these middle-aged people were there in the theater watching it. Beards and glasses. Lapping it up. Until Ryan started yelling about motherfuckers, babyfuckers, fuckersfuckingbabymotherfuckers, and so on. Some middle-aged guy stood up told him to be quiet. Ryan pushed him back down, spilled the Coke and popcorn. The guy's wife became very upset. Henry said it was pretty bad. Said Jerry and Chris, the two brothers who run the place, were not pleased. Jerry and Chris are hippies, but not really. They have long hair, but they also wear red Converse Chuck Taylors, plain t-shirts and their jeans are not flares; pretty

straight actually. More important they like good music, especially Elvis Costello. They really love old Elvis. But best of all they
book lots of great music movies: *DOA, The Harder They Come,
Quadrophenia, Rockers,* and my favourite film of all time, *Rudeboy,*
the Clash movie. So even if Jerry and Chris wore huge flares, had
flowers in their hair and tie-died everything they owned they
would still be OK with me. Most of *Rudeboy* takes place in
Brixton and Shepard's Bush where the Clash are from. I think
those places might be like here. I've never been but I've read all
about it in the *New Musical Express* and *Melody Maker,* but not in
Sounds because *Sounds* is strictly for skinheads. I think the Clash
would like it here. I think about riding the 105 with Paul
Simonon and his hair orange and spiky the way it is on the cover
of the first album. As I think about me and Paul the bus passes
by Prudhomme Avenue where we buy pot, then Villa du (best in
the city!) Souvlaki where we eat, turns down Decarie and pulls
up to Vendome metro station. Mom and I step down and then
another sort of a funny thing happens. We are trying to avoid
the pools of slush that are everywhere, when another bus pulls
up, and almost soaks us in dirty ice water. I jump back and my
mom has to do a quick little run and skip not to get splashed.
Even though I'm mad at the driver, that is sort of hilarious to me,
my Mom bouncing like a gazelle in her church clothes, so I burst
out laughing. Then we are both laughing, standing there in the
slush. That's nice. Having a laugh with my Mom. But really we
should be cursing the bus driver, because he could have avoided
that puddle, and that is pretty terrible, splashing a woman and
her daughter on their way to Mass. That must count as some
kind of terrible sin. But that's people for you, and especially bus

drivers, they'll kick you right in the cunt if you give them half a chance, and if their shoe gets scuffed, they'll ask you for a shine. The metro speeds through the tunnels. At Place D'armes station out we go and there we are. Inside the Cathedral it's all saints waiting with loving wooden arms, shrines with holy canoes, young boys walking by pyramids, golden walls and ceiling, stain-glass David and Goliath, Abraham and Moses, the altar and crosses, candles and incense, organ lurching, and a honey brown light coming off it all. The only thing you can call it is holy, even if you are like me, unsteady in your faith with soul in imminent danger of eternal damnation. The Priest takes his place, there is some singing and then the service begins. As we get closer to Communion I start to get a little worried. That one thought keeps rolling around in my head. The one I have been avoiding. It just plays over and over like the melody of some bad song you hear on the radio, and that song is Henry's cock in my ass, Henry's cock in my ass cock in my ass cock in ass cock ass cock ass cock ass cock ass . . . then Mom tugs my sleeve, time to go. I think about not going. I think about the Clash. Because Paul wouldn't go. I should tell her, sorry Mom, don't really believe in the Holy Roman Catholic Church anymore, so you just go ahead without me. Then just stay here. Minding my own business. Looking at the pretty pictures on the ceiling. But I get up with everyone else and walk to the altar, my soul black and heavy with sins not yet confessed. I bend my knee and prepare to take the body and the blood of Christ. The world is quiet. I wait for the wafer on the tip of my tongue to burst into flames. But it doesn't. It just sits there. Dissolving. One quick swallow and then back to our seats for more singing. I feel a bit sick, but mostly relieved for not having been struck down, consumed in hellfire, etcetera. Soon enough it's back in the metro back across town. We walk out into the cold and look for the 105, but it is nowhere. Across the street the 90 waits. It is not really our bus, as it runs along St. Antoine, on the other side of the railway tracks. But there is an overpass at Grand Avenue, chipped grey cement covered in spray paint, that you take to the other side. It is dark now and still snowing, and I love walking over the trains with the snow and the lights along the tracks, so I tell my Mom we should take the 90, for a change. She worries a bit because usually we take the 105. That's our bus. That is what we usually do. But in the end I convince her and we step on. Once again I start thinking about the Clash, because of that line in *Rudie Can't Fail,* right at the beginning, where Joe Strummer sings: *On the route of the 90 bus!* It used to make us wonder, Bug, Ryan, Henry, Stephen and me, if the Clash had been on our bus, visited when we weren't looking. But then Stephen looked at the lyric sheet one day and said: It's the *19* bus, not the 90 bus. We all looked at it and then had to pretty much agree that the Clash had probably never been to the neighbourhood, or written a song about our bus route. As I think about the Clash the 90 rattles away from the curb. Under a highway overpass. Into white snow. Blue night. By the Italian restaurant where the boys go for steak sandwiches after hockey. By the park that is the Italian kids' park, not really our park, but we still go sometimes to play soccer, or use their pool in the summer. By Beaconsfield Avenue where, on the other side of the tracks, near Monkland, Henry lives with his mom, in an apartment that looks like what people in the nineteen-fifties imagined the future would be. On the overpass the

snow is tumbling slow and thick just like I love, and my Mom
walks beside me as we go up and over to the bottom of our street,
then past our park where kids skate on an outdoor rink, toward
the apartment building at the other side, the one with the tree
in the front yard that's thick with Christmas lights, where I live,
with my Mom, and our Father who art in heaven hallowed be
thy name thy kingdom come thy will be done and I don't know
if you just decided to let me off the hook back there with the
wafer and everything, or don't really care about that kind of
thing, or who knows maybe don't even exist anymore having
gone and left us all alone, but be all that as it may just wanted to
say how much I appreciate not being struck me dead on the spot,
and I for my part swear I will never again take bennies before
mass no matter how late I stay up the night before with Henry
and the anal sex.

DETROIT
St. Andrew's Hall

It's the full-on-hard-core-punk-rock-all-ages show. About fifty bands play before us and about thirty after. When I was fifteen this would have been heaven, now I just have a headache. Band on stage seems very positive, talking between songs about McDonalds sucking facist cops and so on. Anyway good kids, and I start to feel a bit bad because I used to do that, and now, well now, I just take drugs get drunk try to make girls and laugh at kids like this telling them to grow up. While I ruminate on lost ideals the band is raising somewhat different senti-ments with some other audience members. This massive skinhead jumps on stage and punches the lead singer, tiny kid, right in the face. Then the scary bald man grabs the microphone and says: This is America, love it or fucking leave it cocksuckers! . . . ahh Chuck Berry was right, always so good to be back in the USA. At the front of the stage about twenty of his pals nod bald and menacing. The crowd is quiet. Cause really who there is going to tell them different? This is a punk rock show and most of the kids are 98 pounds spent their lives sand kicked in the face. That is why the hair is green and the jeans are torn. I help bloodied tiny singer get backstage. Then go tell the band we have a situation on our hands. Tell them we have to cancel. Get out of here. But Phil says no way we came here to rock the kids and that is what we're going to do. Oh, OK what the fuck do I know? I'm just the roadie. A guy that carries stuff. So I set the stage sit on the sidelines. The band comes on. Kids are cheering. Sara says hello, and that's all. Good good that's very good. Just keep quiet and we may just make it out of here alive. A little drum roll. Off we go. And surprise surprise the show turns out pretty well. Best one of the tour in fact. The band plays with a quiet intensity. The kids jump up and down with the stupid joy of being fifteen. Everybody's happy. After the last song Phil steps up to the microphone, thanks and good night. And I think to myself we made it! But then he asks, you guys like jokes? Yeah, scream the kids. OK, how many skinheads does it take to screw in a light bulb. How many? chant the kids. I can see that the local nazi glee club getting agitated. Two . . . one to bend over and the other to shove his head up his ass. I don't really get it. But the angry bald dudes seem to.

FRENCH PEOPLE SUCK

Frances is asleep beside Henry her head resting against the window. In the seat ahead, Angie Kiamos stands up to get something out of the overhead luggage compartment. Angie has a hint of a mustache. Looking up at her, Henry can see a few black hairs peeking out from her nose. Truth be told, he tells himself, she is sort of hairy all over. And though some call her Angie ape, Henry likes it: soft hairs on her throat that catch the light; forearms with a darker coat; her inner thighs, near the crotch, seen once during gym, tiny ringlets spilling from under her bloomers. Henry dreams of flossing his teeth with those hairs!

Frances mumbles in her sleep and moves her legs. Henry watches her rub her face. When she is settled he turns back to Angie. The overhead is stuck and as she wrestles with it her ass shakes. Henry looks and thinks, one of the world's great asses, and there it is right in front of me. He thinks, I want it, want it so bad I think my cock will break. Watching her stretch, it is all he can do not to reach out for her ass. He sits on his hands to keep them from moving. He worries that he is going to die. That his cock will explode, leaving the bus and all it's passengers covered in white sticky goo, and he, Henry, dead. He thinks I must touch it or I will die. I am going to touch it, I'm going to move my hands and I am going to touch it, so I won't die, and one hand starts to slide from under his leg, when suddenly a voice calls from the seat behind. It's Ryan, reminding them all it is time to get high.

Stephen closes the bathroom door. Frances sits on the sink. Bug on the toilet. Ryan sparks it up, passes it over to Henry, who is by the window. Outside snow covered trees go by. Every winter it's the same goddamn thing he thinks as he inhales deep, they put us on a bus, drag us out to the woods and mess up our heads with the French Canadian country life, part of a class we take at school: *Introduction a la Vie Quebecoise*, because apparently living here isn't quite enough to grasp the concept, apparently you also need to study it. Just then the joint starts to run, interrupting his thoughts. Orange sparks fall onto his pants, and as he is brushing them off, there is a knock on the door. *Qu'est ce que tu fais la?* asks Madame Lise, their teacher, and pretty hot according to Henry, in an older, thin, chain-smoking, bleach-blonde sort of way. They don't say anything. Madame Lise rattles the door. *Qui est la?* she asks. Henry whisper to Frances, tell her it's you. Girls take longer. Frances whispers back, no way. So in a girl's voice he says, *C'est moi, Frances.* Fuck you, real Frances whispers to him and pinches his arm. Hard. *Depechez vous, Frances,* chides Madame Lise from the other side, *il y a d'autres qui attendent. Oui Madame,* Henry answers. They can hear that she doesn't go away. That she is on the other side of the door. Waiting. Stephen pushes by Henry and tries to pry open the window. The rest just stand there looking at each other with the same scared, stupid, stoned grin. The window pops open and fresh air floods in. The handle rattles again, *Frances, Frances?* They are all quiet, especially real Frances. She is not saying a word. Accordingly, Henry replies, *Juste un moment Madame.*

    – *Mais qu'est ce que tu fais, Frances?*

Henry can't think of anything better so lobs, *Je change le tampon, Madame.* They all start snickering. You stupid dick, whispers real Frances, but she is giggling too.

– *Frances? Qu'est ce que tu a dis?*

– *Tampon, tampon, je change le tampon,* he says, *but le tampon est stuck.* Now they are all laughing. Very loud. No point in turning back, so Henry goes, *Est que vous peut help moi avec ma tampon? S'il vous plait Madame. Help moi stick it in?* Ha ha ha ha   Ha   ha   ha   ha

They pull up in front of a chalet. There are already buses in the parking lot. The kids look out the window. There are the other buses, but no people. It's quiet . . . *too* quiet, Henry says. Frances gives a dirty look, tells him to shut up. Jesus, Henry says, it's just a joke. Still angry Madame Lise herds them into the chalet. It's dark inside. Christmas lights flash on the walls. A disco-ball hangs lonely and unused. Tables and chairs are spread out across the room. In one corner there is a pool table and a bunch of video games. They take a table in the darkest corner and send Bug off for mixer. Ryan breaks out the bacardi and soon enough they are sipping delicious breakfast rum & Cokes.

Henry gives the French kids on the other side of the room the once-over and says, Oh my God, what a group of pepsi-drinking, mae West-eating, hockey-haircut-sporting country hicks. By the juke-box a few of them are standing around punching in songs and having a sing along. They are in the middle of

Breakfast In America. The boys slide down in their seats, sip their drinks and laugh laugh laugh. . . . *Could we have kippers for breakfast?* All much too fucking funny. And look, there is one whose hockey-hair is the longest, whose Lois jeans are the tightest, the King Pepper, and he is leading them in song. And you know it's all for our benefit, thinks Henry, the way they keep playing it up and looking over. They are showing off for us. And that just makes it funnier. Silly hicks . . . Supertramp are gay. Go back to screwing cows, you stupid farmers. But not just yet, because this is *too* funny. God, French people totally suck, Henry laughs.

– Don't be so racist, says Frances just back from the bathroom.

– It's not my fault they're a bunch of hicks, Henry tell her.

– Sometimes you are such an asshole, Henry, Frances says.

– Yeah, Henry, agrees Bug, sometimes you are such an asshole.

– Shut up, retard, and Henry throws an empty Coke can at him. Go practice for your career being a garbage-man. Bug limply replies that actually it is Henry who's going to be a garbage-man. So Henry asks why did Bug get fired from his job at the sperm-bank?

– Why? asks Ryan.

– Drinking on the job. So ha-ha Bug drinks sperm. So Bug throws the can back. So Henry throws it at him. So Bug throws it back at Henry. So the morning goes.

Exiting the bathroom Henry sees her. The disco ball now spins, and throws shafts of light that dance over her flipped hair, across her tight sweater. She takes a pack of cigarettes from her jacket pocket, and as she puts one to her lips their eyes meet. Henry's mouth goes dry. They stare at each other. A horrible Journey song starts . . . *It's a long night . . . All night.* She pulls out a lighter and she starts for the back door. Henry glances over to where Frances and Ryan are playing Ms. Pac Man, then makes for that back door as fast as he can.

Outside he can't see her. He spins round looking. Then hears a whistle, and from behind the far corner, she is waving. They take a path that can't be seen from the chalet, into the trees, where little buckets hang from trunks collecting sap. After walking a bit, they stop for a rest on a bench behind the barn, well out of chalet sight. At first all Henry can do is look at her body. Sure they talk, but he is completely focused on glances at breasts trapped by a bra that glows black from inside a thin yellow sweater; at the gap between that yellow sweater and the blue jeans where her white stomach puckers up and overflows its tight wrapping; at the thighs she keeps crossing.

Then a funny thing happens. The more they talk, the more he starts to listen, and the more he starts to listen, the more his heart starts to sing three little sounds: Anne-Ma-Rie! She tells him about her family and about her boyfriend (doesn't like them). About her school and her friends (doesn't like them either). About her hopes and dreams (to be a singer). About her plans to move to New York City (if you can make it there). Henry tries to explain that big cities are hard. That it is tough. I can do anything, she says and sticks out her tongue and looks so pretty Henry thinks forget New York, move to Montreal instead. We could live with my Mom for a while, then find a place of our own. We could get jobs after school. It would be hard, but we'd make it. He asks about favourite bands; favourite movies; do they have *The White Shadow* in French; what she was like when she was five; and they are laughing and having fun, things going very well, so he asks her if she gets high, and when she doesn't seem to get it, shows her the joint in his cigarette pack. She smiles and takes his hand.

They slip inside the barn. After the smoking, a little bit of kissing starts. Henry wasn't really thinking about that anymore, so it catches him by surprise. We don't have to, he tells her. But she just throws her tongue back into his mouth. So Henry touches her tits, rolls a nipple through sweater bra, his hands slide over her ass, inside her pants, under panties, fingers traveling across frosty cheeks, between goosed inner thighs, before parting pussy lips backwards. His cock is now very hard, and she is rubbing it, and he tries to move her into place, up against one of the sugaring-off tables, but she shakes her head. Too cold, she says. Too cold? he asks. I'm very cold, she answers. We can warm each other up, says kissing Henry. No, she shakes her head. And Henry can see her breath. And he has to admit that his fingers are going numb. And his face hurts. And he can't feel his feet. And he curses this country. He curses his parents. He curses the fur-trappers, explorers, missionaries and all the other stupid bastards that founded this fucked, frozen nation. Defeated and dejected, he leans against the sugaring off table, and about to light a cigarette he has a vision: The Bus.

They sneak around the side of the barn, and are waiting for the best chance to cross the parking lot, when they are startled from behind. Henry turns to find a very angry young man he recognizes as the King Pepper, the ringleader from the Super-tramp sing-along, but who Anne-Marie knows as Pierre, her boyfriend of three and a half years. Pierre starts yelling and screaming. Anne-Marie starts crying. Henry is wondering what to do, when Pierre says something he can't quite understand, but the general meaning seems very clear, as Pierre's fists are curling and he is moving quick, so Henry answers with a punch to the face, pretty hard, though not hard enough, as Pierre hits him right back. Henry is reeling, and just able to hit Pierre again. In return Pierre really smacks Henry. The world is spinning. Henry swings blindly, lands a lucky one and Pierre's nose pops open. Henry gets his bearings, sees Pierre is distracted by the blood squirting from between the fingers held to his face, thinks he might just get out of this in one piece, when a hard knock comes from behind. Ears ringing, Henry turns toward the blow . . . oh Anne-Marie, how could you? What about our little apartment? Our after-school jobs? What about us? She hits him again, right under his left eye. Then both of them are hitting him. Then all the other kids are spilling out from the chalet and a bench-clearing brawl erupts in the parking lot. Kids are smashing each other. Teachers are breaking it up. Over by the barn one kid gets smacked, falls back onto a sugaring-off table, blood soaking the fresh snow.

The bus pulls out of the parking lot and makes for the highway. Madame Lise so angry she sits by the bus driver, smoking ciga-rette after cigarette, and the kids too scared to make even a crack. Henry is in back stretched out on a pair of seats. Frances is beside him holding a cloth against the cut under his eye. She asks, what happened? So Henry tells her, I went outside for a cigarette. A French kid was yelling at his girlfriend. So I told him to take it easy, and the guy hit me. Then his girlfriend hit me. Then they both started knocking the hell out of me. Just like that. For nothing. No reason at all. Frances pushes the hair back from his forehead. Poor baby, she says, and then, you were right, French people do suck. Henry just nods his head and pretends that it doesn't hurt.

DAYTON
Stache's

Tim's asleep in our room. I drop by Phil and Chuck's to let them know
what time we're going to the show. Chuck is in the bathtub reading.
He got the worst of the fight. We were worried his hand was broken,
but we went to the hospital and it's just bruised. I tell him to ice it after
the bath. OK mom, he says. Phil is on one of the beds noodling on his
guitar watching TV. I tell him we're going over to sound check at eight.
That's two hours, so you try to stay out of trouble till then, OK killer.
I'll try, he says. Then it's off to Sara's room. I always get nervous when
I talk to her. Always have and now even more since our relationship
suffered that unfortunate set back last tour when I took acid and con-
fessed to her about sleeping with a prostitute in Amsterdam. She was
very understanding, but I know that she thinks less of me now. Sara is
pretty punk and doesn't care much for guys who sleep with hookers. At
least I wasn't so high that I told her about those two at the same time
German girls in Munich, or Natalie out in the east end, or any of those
others. She'd hate me for sure if she knew about all that. Whatever.
We all have our little secrets and if you're smart you keep them that
way. That night the band plays not half bad. Not as good as the night
before but you can almost remember how hard they used to rock. Too
bad only about fifty people are there to see it. After I'm sitting at the
bar with Tim. I talked to Alison last night, he mentions. You ever call
that girl Gidget? No, I say, haven't called her. We have another round.

ICE VS. FIRE

Ryan is perched on the edge of the boards of the outdoor rink smoking a cigarette when the kid skates up and says, You played for St. Kevin's.

– What?

– You're Ryan Pearse, and you played for St. Kevin's.

– Yeah, so?

– The year we won. You played.

– Yeah, so?

– So, that was awesome. The last game with North Shore. You scored the winner in overtime.

– Yeah, yeah, I did.

Henry skates up and takes the cigarette pack. He looks at Ryan. He looks at the kid. Who's the kid?

– Don't know. What's your name kid?

– Chris, says the kid.

– You want a smoke Chris? asks Henry.

– Sure, answers the kid, and Henry passes him one, and they sit there smoking with the kid going on about the big hockey star Ryan used to be, which Ryan especially enjoys because Henry is there to hear. Henry, of course, played hockey, but was never good enough for inter-city, so has to sit nodding, that's great, wow, that is just so great.

Soon enough Henry skates off, and the kid starts on going out for the team himself, in a couple of years of course, when he's older, and how he's pretty sure he'll make it because Father

Tom has been scouting him, and though it's a long ways off, has already told him, confidentially, that if he keeps developing the way he's been, well then, it's practically in the bag. Ryan watches the little kid talking, sees that he hasn't even shaved yet, lips and mouth like a small girl, and he starts to feel sick.

Just then Henry passes by, and makes a big show of winding up for a big slap shot. Wood and ice and hard rubber come together. Ryan and the kid watch the puck sail through the air, over the net, over the boards, across the snow, out into the dark. They watch where the puck goes, and though they cannot exactly see that small black disk moving through the big black night, they can follow the general path, and what they see there, under the park light, is a man pulling his child on a toboggan, on their way home, both tired from a hard day on the slopes, and then the father drops to the ground, like he has been shot by a sniper. Ryan turns to the kid: Holy shit, I think he hit him!

The boys run skate across the snow covered football field, from the outdoor rink to the park path where a child sits on a toboggan looking at his father, who is stretched out unconscious on the snow, blood dripping from a gash on his forehead, and the small piece of hard black rubber lies nearby, half-hidden in the white, now apparently harmless. Not even Stephen knows what to do, so he stands there with Ryan, Henry and Bug waiting for something to happen, which it luckily does, when one of the park attendants, who was hosing down the girl's rink and saw the whole thing, comes running. He presses a hand-full of snow wrapped in a scarf to the father's head and sends Ryan off to the comfort station to call for an ambulance.

By the time father, son and ambulance are gone it is after seven. The boys skate the rink; Chris the kid also gone home. Henry winds up for one last shot, and the other three hit the ice . . . ha ha ha very fucking funny, he thanks them. Down in the comfort station they loosen their skates, frosty needles jabbing toes as feet thaw out. Clumps of ice are scraped from frozen blades and then hurled across the room with a loud joke, but Ryan just dumps his ice at this feet and says almost nothing, the image of the little boy sitting all alone on the toboggan floating in his lonely thoughts.

At home his mother is angry, she has made pork chops (Ryan's favourite!), and he is late, but dinner hasn't been completely ruined, so it is all right. As they eat, Ryan tells her the story, and when he comes to the part about the small boy sitting all alone on the dark path, tears well up in his eyes. Oh honey, his mother comforts as she wraps her arms around him. A bit later, when they are watching TV, his mother brings him a bowl of ice cream, vanilla with butterscotch ripple. Curled up on the sofa they watch the rest of M*A*S*H, all of Tootsie, and the first half of Saturday Night Live.

The next day, his mother gone to work, Ryan wanders the apartment, then pulls on his boots, zips his jacket, puts on his hat and scarf, and opens the front door. Few people are out. The world is soft, empty, white, as he makes his way to the local police station. It's been awhile, but he recognizes the front desk. The police officer looks up from his newspaper. *Bonjour*, he asks.

– Hi.

– So, what can I do for you?

– I want to report a crime.

– What kind of crime?

– Sex crime. Adults against kids. That kind.

– OK, well why don't you take a seat, someone will be out to talk with you in a minute. The officer exits through a door that leads deeper into the station, and, presumably, to the person who will be out in a minute to talk. Ryan is alone in the lobby. He looks around. The marble floors are speckled pale industrial green. The row of padded chairs is light blue. The table that breaks that line of light blue is brown, and the lamp orange, and a terror is starting deep in his heart, jumping straight to his lungs, and they start beating in and out like a small bird trapped in a plastic bag, like cracking billows stoking the fire that is burning him alive, and every nerve is white hot, every cell drowning in flames, and all he can think is oh god I am dying I am dying oh god I am dying and this burning pulls him under while outside the front doors the world is still there, the snow is still falling, and on the way down the steps Ryan almost slips, the grey sky thundering toward him like a hundred thousand horses, coming in from all directions, with the thick white flakes swirling, and he grabs at the handrail for balance, staggers the rest of the way down, now bent over, now gasping for air, now the cold clean filling his lungs, now just keep breathing just keep walking breathing walking breathing walking till it all so slowly sinks down far enough that he can light a cigarette. Then it is back to slinking quietly along sidewalks, down empty darkening streets, to his apartment building, home in plenty of time for dinner, mom making spaghetti with meatballs (Ryan's second favourite!). After, his mom watches TV while Ryan finishes up the dishes; he leaves the water running for cover, and opens her purse to fish out enough for beer and a fifth.

Back in the park Ryan sits on a bench, just to the left of the rink. The big lights are now off and all is quiet, the snow has stopped and the moon is shining on the clean white that stretches to the dark trees, and it is so cold his cigarettes taste like menthols, and the scotch so cheap it burns like gonorrhea, and he sits there so long he finds himself wandering the halls of his elementary school, through the old cloak room decorated with paint, glitter and macaroni, to the small bathroom at the back, where a voice asks for some tissue, and he passes it over the door, which then opens and there is Cindy Clark, straight blonde hair held back by a blue beret, blue dress, blue shoes, and she kisses him thanks on the mouth, then turns into Father Tom, at which point Ryan luckily wakes, because you could die on a park bench, in Montreal, sleeping through the winter.

COLUMBUS
Peabody's

The kid sitting outside watching me load in asks how I got my big fat start in the punk rock equipment movement sector, and I tell him here carry this, tell him it was the music man, it was all for the music, tell him how none of my friends would start a band with me, so I started playing with some fellows I didn't know all that well, and how we were the absolute worst brokenblenderpunkjunk you have ever heard, but I wanted to be in a band so much that I just kept at it. How our rehearsal space was in an old building that was falling apart, but for some reason had leaves glued to all the ceilings, so people called it The Forest. How Phil and Sara and Tim were just starting up, and they were in the room next to us. Chuck didn't join till the next year, and they had a guy called Brian playing guitar, and even back then they were so good. I would hang around just to watch them practice. It was like watching greasy teenage Vincent Van Goghs painting on toilet paper, like fireworks in the afternoon, like the most important thing ever but only seven people knew about it, and they were drunk. I hung around so much that we got friendly and when they started getting shows, I helped out, driving, loading in, doing stage. They kept getting bigger and better and it turned into a more full-time thing. Around the same time it was getting pretty clear that I was never going to make it as a rock star, so I put away the hair spray, hung up my guitar, and became a roadie. Been living the high life ever since.

HOCKEY NIGHT IN QUÉBEC

Every spring, thinks Stephen, it's the same. The snow melts, and then we're in the playoffs. This year we beat Boston in three for the Adams' semis, Bug, the die-hard Bruins fan, cries in his beer, Henry, the good sport, dances around in a circle. Then it's a battle with Hartford for the division finals, but we triumph 4-3. The Rangers roll over in five for the Wales Conference and that brings us to the big show: the Stanley Cup. We drop the first game in Calgary – end of the world, much weeping and wailing and gnashing of teeth – then take the next four straight to victory; the hopes and prayers of the faithful are rewarded; oh Joy, oh sweet sweet Joy. On the TV Guy Carbonneau hoists the cup over his head. The rest of the team pump their arms in the air, skate in circles, jump all over each other, laugh and shout, as an arena full of glum Calgarians look on from the stands.

Back in Montreal, at Bug's apartment, the kids dance around the room. Henry leans into the TV and screams at the distant, flickering images: BETTER LUCK NEXT YEAR, YOU COWBOY FAGGOTS! Dick Irvin, the voice of the Canadiens, is saying, raise another banner in the Forum, 23rd cup in the glorious Habs' dynasty, the most successful sports franchise in the history of the planet! The kids keep jumping, singing the good-bye song that is sung at the end of the game your team wins; even Bug gets caught up in the moment and joins in, when, on the TV the crying cowboys are replaced by shots of downtown Montreal, where the streets are filled with people, and Dick is saying, not since the days of Maurice Richard's suspension by Mr. Clarence Campbell and the ensuing riots have we seen this kind of nonsense on the streets of Montreal. The kids all quiet down. On the TV people are filling up St. Catherine's Street, cheering, singing, drinking, milling about. Seems peaceful enough. But small fires burn in trashcans, then the sound of breaking glass, and then a louder, thicker noise from off camera, and the crowd surges forward. The TV cuts to a commercial. Henry picks up the phone. We need a cab, he says. Stephen asks him, where are we going?

– Where the fuck do you think? he says.

The cabbie won't take them any further than Sherbrooke and Atwater, so out they go. Walking down Atwater, past the Alexis Nihon Plaza, there is not much traffic. The few cars are moving slowly, or stopped in the middle of the street, their drivers looking around nervously. Ahead the kids can see people streaming along St. Catherine's. They cover the sidewalks and the road. They are walking on parked cars. They are up on the roofs of buildings. The night air is pocked with yells and shouts, and underneath it all the steady low roll of mob thunder. Stephen watches his friends dive right in. Henry has his arm wrapped around Frances as they move down the sidewalk seemingly back together this week. Bug ducks into a dep and comes out with six-packs. Beer, for all my friends, he says. Ryan, already stumbling, takes two. Henry sips and looks around eyes wide like a kid at the foot of a monster roller coaster. This is so fucking excellent, he says. And Stephen has to admit to the feelings' tug. You can almost hear the amusement park music, smell peanuts and cotton candy, the whirl of the rides, the hot neon flash of it all.

At the corner of Guy they see the first car flip. A gang gathered around a Honda Civic rocking it from one side to the other. Then it is half over, and everyone yelling yelling out of the way out of the way out of the way, as the crowd pulls back, and the car tumbles onto its roof, where it spins like an upset beetle. A bus has turned up St. Marc and on to St. Catherine's. The driver leans on the horn, but the crowd just swarms tighter, and the bus starts to rock. A cop car is coming to the rescue, the siren going as they try to make their way through to the lonely, wobbling bus, but the crowd is not parting. The cop car is stopped. It starts to rock as well. The crowd grabs for the lights and the siren. They are tearing them off the roof. The neutered cop car slinks down Bishop, while the bus teeters, then crashes onto its side, and the crowd rushes together calling out for more. Stephen thinks of his mother and father at home watching on television: father shakes his head and says to mother, they're crazy; mother agrees, I think we've seen enough; they switch off the TV and go upstairs to bed. Stephen looks over at Henry, Bug, Ryan and their faces are exploding with delight as they watch the cop car leave. For them it's like Christmas, sex, pot and free alcohol all rolled into one.

Small fires are burning up and down the street. The crowd is squeezed shoulder to shoulder between the shops that line both sides. Then from halfway down the block comes the sound of breaking glass. The kids turn their heads and see people are streaming out of a corner dep with cigarettes, wine, beer, bread, donuts, etc. Then they see a shoe shop go down. An electronics store. A book store. Then a brick is tossed at the clothing boutique right across the street from them. The glass shakes like a gong, but holds. People start yelling at the twelve-year-old brick tosser telling him to do it. Grown men and women shouting: DO IT DO IT DO IT! The kid walks up to the window. Picks up the brick. He walks back a few steps. The crowd chants. The kid looks at the brick. The window. Then real quick goes into a full wind-up. This time it sails straight through. Glass falls to the sidewalk in a crackling rain. A short, quiet moment. Then the crowd gushes forward. Henry jumps up. Come on! he says. Ryan and Bug are right there with him. Wait a second, says Stephen and then, because it's the only thing he can think of, adds, it isn't right. They look at him for a second, puzzled, like he had suddenly started talking about European history, then, without another word, charge across the street.

The three storm right in, while Frances and Stephen stop a few feet shy of where the window had been. Stephen thinks of his parents lying in bed at home. Safe and sound. Inside the store clothes are being thrown everywhere. Mannequins are falling. People are falling. Stephen is standing out on the sidewalk with Frances peering into the dark. This can't be right, he thinks to himself, it may feel good, but can't be right. Then another part says, you are a gutless pussy. To which the first side replies, why bother with looting, let's move right to the rape and murder. The answer, you are an accountant waiting to happen. Counterpoint: decency and respect still count for something. Point: pussy. Counterpoint: but they do. Point: pussy pussy pussy. It goes back and forth like that, with Stephen teetering on the edge. Ryan and Henry emerge, drop more loot on the sidewalk, and are just about to dive back in, when the sirens start. From side streets, cops

decked out in full riot gear wade into the crowd. Lights are flashing. Bug comes bolting out of the store, and that's everyone, so
they make a break for it run run run up Bishop, trailing discarded
plunder behind. At Sherbrooke they turn, look back down the
street where little bonfires glow and the crowd fights the police.
From there it looks like TV with the sound down low.

The long walk home starts with a large joint. Very stoned Stephen
listens to his friends laugh about the excellent riot. The streets go
by. The night gets quieter, broken by the occasional passing of a
tardy police car racing to the action. Then, as if, thinks Stephen,
this evening hasn't been strange enough, they come up on St.
Kevin's and there is Father Tom standing outside on the steps, in
housecoat and slippers, presumably trying to take the troubled
city's ethical temperature. Evening, he says, heard there was a little trouble downtown. Yeah, a little trouble, Stephen listens to his
friends mumble. He watches them stand there with their heads
bowed, like the sidewalk has suddenly become incredibly fascinating, watches Ryan beside him so nervous he starts to shake.
It's hard to know, thinks Stephen, the things that will bother
them. Rampaging and pillaging seem fine, but seeing a priest
when you're stoned, now that's real trouble. Stephen watches as
Father Tom chats a bit more, seemingly oblivious to the reaction
he is provoking in his young flock. Finally he says, see you on
Sunday, which makes Stephen laugh because it has been years
since any of them have seen the inside of a church. Yeah sure,
Sunday, their eyes still glued to their shoes. As they stumble off
Stephen thinks it's like some weird hangover from their parents'

world, they never got close enough to understand the rules or feel the joy, missed out on the mercy, the miracles and the love, and now all that's left is a bit of guilt, a little fear and some really filthy nun jokes.

At Westmount Park they stop for a rest. Smoke more pot as they soak their feet in the wading pool. Lean back and stare up at the stars. Look, the big dipper. Venus. A satellite. Ryan tumbles into the pool and swims a few laps in the waist-deep water. With all the grace of a drunken garbage collector he starts to climb the statue in the middle. Miraculously he makes it to the top, where he swings, just barely holding on. Stephen looks at him up there, dumb and wasting away, and starts to feel a low-down depression crawling in. What used to be fun is now no fun, and just feels stupid, and he wonders how did that happen: how did we get to be so stupid, how did we ever get to be the stupidest of all . . . when up on the statute Ryan slips and almost falls. Hey Ryan, calls Frances, why don't you come down now. Nah, I'm OK, is the answer. Henry, he's not OK, says Frances, do something. Henry wades into the pool, hey Ryan come on down. But Ryan won't. So Henry climbs halfway up the statue and tries to grab hold. He catches a leg. Gets Ryan by the waist, starts dragging, and slowly the two descend the statue. All of a sudden Ryan pushes off and they are falling, out in the air, tumbling from the statue, a penny and a feather, through the night, to the water. Before they can even wonder if the two are dead, Ryan and Henry are up, their arms around each other's necks in dueling headlocks. They tip over again. Then back up. Now Ryan is punching Henry and Henry is punching Ryan and they are all jumping into the pool trying to break it up. The two are staggering around in the water.

Ryan's nose is bloody. He is saying, I'm OK, I'm OK, I'm OK. Henry is disagreeing, you got a serious fucking problem, mother-fucker! Ryan's answer, to what seems to Stephen a pretty accurate assessment, is to rip off his shirt and run around the park yelling Jesus loves me at the top of his lungs. The others stand there watching him sprint back and forth over grass. Going nowhere. Shirt off. Soaking wet. Bloodied face. Screaming nonsense junk. They look at each other. What is this? What are we going to do? Eventually he calms down and Frances has him sit on a bench with her. He curls up and puts his head in her lap. The boys sit on another bench smoking. When the sky starts to turn from black to blue, it's time to go. Stephen heads up the hill to his Westmount home, and the others keep on the walk west to NDG.

The next morning Stephen feels terrible. Hangover clouding his head he lies in bed thinking about his friends. They were supposed to play ball hockey behind the high school, but Stephen doubts it after last night. So he lies in bed a bit longer. Eventually gets up, walks downstairs to the kitchen, and pours a cup of coffee. His father is at the table reading the paper. Stephen sits down to a bowl of Cheerios, and starts to eat. His father looks at him. Did you enjoy yourself last night? he asks. It was OK, didn't do much, he mumbles. Oh, don't be so modest. I just want you to know that your mother and I are both very proud. Then he passes the paper across the table. Underneath the caption "Fans Ruin Perfect Cup Win" is a big picture of Ryan and Henry stepping out of the store their hands full of clothes. And there is Stephen, right behind them, eyes wide, looking out at the world.

PHILADELPHIA
Crocadero's

The first time we played here someone broke in the van and stole all our stuff. All we had left was the gear and the clothes we were wearing. Spent the rest of the tour in Salvation Army dresses and Goodwill slacks. Now I pay the guy who says he will watch the van for us: ten now and ten later. End of the evening, and tired of dingy rock bars, I want to go to this dingy strip-bar nearby. There is a girl I met last time, and I like her, and I'd like to see her again. Also, I'd like to see her tits. Unfortunately, Tim is off somewhere, and I don't want to go alone, so I ask Chuck, though I should know better. Right away he starts with his "You are a victim of porno" routine. Save it dad, I tell him. Chuck has explained his porno theory so many times I could write the book: We live in a porno world and the point of everything we see and hear, movies, records, commercials, videos, radio, whatever, is used to keep us in a state of perpetual and continuous unsatisfied desire, because since we can't ever get laid enough to scratch that itch, we buy stuff instead, and we keep on buying the stuff trying to put out the fire that porno has lit in our hearts, but we can't ever put it out because there is no end to porno desire and so we always want more and more and more and more and more of something we've never even had, because that something actually doesn't even exist. Chuck will usually end it, like he does now, by slamming his fist down on the bar and saying, they want you to be unsatisfied and miserable, because miserable, unsatisfied people make the best consumers . . . they are ruining your life just so they can sell you shit!! USELESS SHIT!! DON'T YOU

FUCKING GET IT!! DOESN'T THAT PISS YOU OFF!!! Yeah yeah dude whatever, like I don't know all that stuff already . . . and it doesn't hardly change the fact that I'd like to see that girl's tits.

HEART LIKE A TOAD

Ryan stares at the ceiling thinks I hate that they wake us at SEVEN most mornings I STAY IN bed longer have a smoke watch Chris arrange his magazines and the things on his desk. After HE is done with the magazines and the desk he puts EVERYTHING on his side of the room in ORDER. At seven thirty the nurse comes in with our MEDS. She carries the MEDS on a tray with a jug of water. The MEDS come in a small plastic cup with your name written on it. Once they are down your day is pretty much SET. I spend most of MINE in MY room. The room I share with Chris. Besides the arranging there are some other problems with him, for example, the smoking. He holds his cigarette A CER-TAIN way, perched between his fingers as if each DRAG were some big event. Just smoke the FUCKING thing, I tell HIM. He only looks at ME, lifts it to his mouth and slowly takes another PUFF. Then there is the walking. He shuffles from place to place, barely lifting his feet OFF the ground with his slippers scuffing on the floor. Sitting in our room, I can hear him start out in the TV room. Scuff scuff, scuff scuff, coming down the hall, getting closer CLOSER, till he rounds the corner and COMES in like he is carrying the weight of the world on his skinny shoulders. Jesus, you are one depressing bastard, I tell him. He just looks at ME and shakes his head before shuffling over to his bed and crawling under covers. But worst of all is the music. Chris will only listen to THE Doors. The same songs OVER and over again and again. When I first arrived I felt BAD for him and lent him my copy of the first Black Flag album but he wouldn't even listen to it, which only goes to show that some people don't WANT to get better. But enough of that here is what happens with THE doors. Chris puts a cassette into HIS tape deck and sits THERE listening with eyes closed. When it is done he rewinds the tape and starts all OVER. It can GO on for HOURS. He even copies the lyrics into his SPECIAL book. He carries the book around with him and sometimes will read from it. We will be watching television and he will open UP the book and say: the killer's head is thumping like a toad. Then STARE at you, like there is some answer he is waiting for. Like there is SOMETHING to say about THAT. On other days he just sits in the corner whispering: break on through break on through break on through . . . so one day WHILE he was listening to THE END for that hundredth time I jumped out of bed, dashed across the room, took the tape OUT and stomped on it. He looked at me sadly and said, Jim died for YOUR SINS. It was all I could do NOT to pick up that tape deck and smash HIS HEAD right in. BUT musical differences aside IT gets pretty boring around here. Not much to DO. Since that time Henry and Bug were here, and that thing happened with the coffee machine, I haven't been allowed any visitors except FAMILY. My mom comes everyday after work, but I feel so awful having her see me LIKE this that I usually just sit there and can't THINK of much to say except so SORRY never do it again all A big big mistake didn't REALLY want to die just kept eating the pills and that much is true picked up twenty figured I'd sell fifteen at the party to cover my FIVE but in the kitchen just kept popping them in my mouth so don't EVEN know what happened after AT ALL don't really know what to say except sorry Mom so SO

SORRY and hope she understands. I really hope so. I bet she DOES. I hope. Anyway, as I was saying, except for Mom coming by, and ping-ponging, television and cigarettes and, of course, waiting for the MEDS there is not much to do. Pretty dull. So I started to move Chris's things around. Sometimes a pencil from the left side of his desk to the right, mix up his socks, or put his chair up on his bed, just to see what would HAPPEN. But Chris was always very collected about it. He played it very COOL, never let on that anything was wrong, just shuffled around the room in his slip slippers putting things back in order. Then, one day, I forget which, I was sitting in bed reading a comic. I heard Chris come in. He walked over and sat down on the edge of MY bed. After FIVE or six pages Chris cleared HIS throat. I looked up. His face was red and the TEARS welling up in HIS eyes were about to spill down HIS cheeks. His hands were laid out palms down BESIDE him on the bed and HIS arms were shaking.

– What's up Chris? I asked.

– What's up . . . What's up . . . I'll tell you what's up, he stuttered while balling up the blanket in his fists. You've been moving my things around, that's what's up. And I just want you to know that I think you are a . . . Total . . . Fucking . . . Asshole!

– Chris, I don't know what you're talking about. I didn't move shit, now get the fuck off of my bed. I opened my COMIC and started reading again. After a few pages I heard him shuffle OUT of the room. I continued on with the mighty Thor, it was still pretty good, BUT interrupted by THOUGHTS of Chris, of that time we played Scrabble, the way HE gave ME his dessert, sound of his BREATHING at night, etcetera . . .

I found Chris in the TV room watching a soap OPERA. Sat down on the couch beside HIM and watched for a bit. A girl was CRYING. She had hidden in the CLOSET and seen her HUSBAND in bed with her mom. Sure makes our troubles seem small, I said to Chris but he didn't laugh. He didn't EVEN answer.

– Look, I'm sorry. I'll never do it again. Chris still DIDN'T say anything. He just continued to watch the television.

– Come on. What do you say?

– I was always nice. Never did a thing wrong to you.

– Yeah, I know.

– So, why did you do it? . . . Why did I do it? Why did I do it? Why DID I do IT? Why DID I DO it? WHY DID I DO IT? OH, I'LL TELL YOU WHY MOTHERFUCKER . . . HE WOULD TELL ME TO BE THERE, AND I WOULD GO, SCARED, HIDING, PRAYING NO ONE WOULD SEE. BUT DIDN'T YOU WANT PEOPLE TO SEE, TO KNOW, SO IT WOULD STOP? THAT'S WHAT THEY WILL ASK. BUT NO! MOTHERFUCKERS NO! YOU DIDN'T WANT PEOPLE TO SEE. NO ONE COULD SEE. NO ONE COULD KNOW. BECAUSE, YOU SEE, MOTHERFUCKERS, THEY ALREADY KNEW. BUT WHY DIDN'T YOU JUST NOT GO. BECAUSE YOU HAD TO GO. YOU COULDN'T JUST NOT GO. AND YOU CAN TELL THAT TO PEOPLE BUT THEY WON'T UNDERSTAND. BECAUSE THERE IS NOTHING TO UNDERSTAND. BECAUSE DEEP IN THE BOTTOM OF OUR DUSTY HEARTS WE ALL ALREADY KNOW. AND SO THERE IS NOTHING TO TELL. AND SO WE ALL KEEP QUIET, AND THOUGH THE REASONS CHANGE IT'S IMPOSSIBLE, UNHEARD OF, FOR ATTENTION, MONEY, IN THE HEAD, MADE UP, CRYING SHAME, NATIONAL EPIDEMIC, ON OPRAH, TIRED . . . BORING

. . . JOKE . . . THE SILENCE ALWAYS REMAINS THE SAME
MOTHERFUCKERS BECAUSE WE ALL ALWAYS DO NOT GIVE
ONE SINGLE FUCK SO MOTHERFUCKERS THERE IS NOTHING
TO DO SO I DID NOTHING MOTHERFUCKERS SO I DID NOTH-
ING . . . so Chris put his hand on my silent, shaking shoulder
and said, it's OK, maybe we can talk about it later. Then he took
his cigarettes out. He lit us UP, the meds started kicking in HARD,
and smoke whispered toward the ceiling, while Chris and me
WE sat quiet on that couch TV watching for the rest of April, all
of MAY, and the first two weeks of June.

PITTSBURGH
Graffiti's

It's a pretty long drive to Pittsburgh. Longer than it seems. Outside the gas stations and the highway signs slip by while the moon turns the world silver. Inside everyone is sound asleep. I don't know what it is, the night, the moon, the highway, or me, but I do something I haven't done in awhile. I slip off my shoe then take off my sock. I turn around to make sure everyone is really sleeping then I undo my pants and pull out my dick, give a few pulls till it's half-hard, then slip my sock over it and start to beat off. I flip through the old rolodex of girls I have known, five seconds each, even think of my old friend Frances, on a diving board, which is weird, then halfway through I hit on Gidget and get stuck. Two good pulls and I'm there as the wheels roll over the asphalt and the night drifts and it is . . . Oh Gidget baby baby . . . then off with the sock down with the window and out it goes. I'm lighting a cigarette when I hear, You got another one of those? Nearly jump out of my skin. Jesus, Sara you scared the fuck out of me. Sorry, she says. One of what? I ask. A cigarette dumb-ass, what do you think? Right, and pass her a smoke as she climbs into the passenger seat. So, you just get up? I ask. Yeah, she says, had a weird dream. About what? Can't recall. So we sit and smoke and watch the road at night. After a bit she asks, You ever wonder where you're heading Bug? Naww . . . we're going to Pittsburgh, I tell her, but it's not that funny.

ABOVE US UFOs ARE FLYING

Frances sees the apartment building, the pool and the dark swimmers. She is sitting on a bench by the edge of the water. The moon shines bright. The pool is surrounded on three sides by a fence. On the fourth side, where there is no fence, there is a wooden cabana and the ground is covered with patio stones; past the patio stones there is grass; past the grass stands the apartment building stretching up into the night sky.

The others are all in the pool. At first they were trying to be quiet, but now, since no one has come, they are laughing and yelling. When they jump off the diving board they try to splash her. The beer in her hand is warm, leaning toward hot, but she takes a drink off it every now and then, just for something to do. It foams up the neck of the bottle and tastes strong at the back of her throat.

– Frances, why don't you come in? calls Henry.

– Just opened a beer, she says but thinks, fuck off. So she sits and watches. The moon makes it easy. Near the diving board Denise stands clutching her breasts, her arms crossed as if she were cold. Close by another girl pulls her hair back and wrings the water out. She is leaning on one leg talking to the boy next to her. Frances watches her do this. She watches the girl watch the boy watch her. I know that one, thinks Frances, I've done that one before.

Near the diving board Ryan drops a bottle. Careful, he says, broken glass, watch out. He bends down and tries to sweep it into the bushes with a cigarette pack. Poor Ryan, Frances keeps on, fresh out of hospital and he is right stupid back where he started, half-naked, dripping wet, cigarette in mouth, wasted, dumb-ass. She tries to get him to talk about it, but he just makes a big joke, telling her he thought it was a handful of mints not quaaludes, telling her he was surprised as anyone to wake up stomach pumped in hospital, telling her his extended stay was part of a top-secret government project to contact alien civilizations with mental telepathy, and that he has been sworn to secrecy, and can never ever discuss it. You spend your whole life with people, thinks Frances, and half the time it feels like you don't even know them. Henry yells again and she doesn't bother to answer him.

Frances could tell from the moment the girl took off her clothes and dove into the water. She could tell the way his eyes were pulled over, even though he was sitting right beside her. And then after a minute how he jumped up saying it is so hot and followed her in. She watched as they swam the length of the pool, their bodies wobbling shadows underneath the surface; as they rested at the edge; as they kicked to the bottom for that quarter and stayed down so long. She wanted to tell him, Henry, you are in water, idiot, you are in the water, and we can all see. But she didn't. They are both drunk and they think that this is exciting. Frances wonders why they still bother. It is hard to get mad, but she is trying.

It's a funny moment, she thinks, when it begins, when you first feel that hand or hip, shoulder or leg. Often they start with the leg, a slight pressure against the thigh, or a shin knocking softly on the back of the calf, maybe the hand on a knee. Earlier that evening, at the bar, Henry had been sitting next to her, talking to someone else. Then his hand was there, between his leg and hers, like an accident. Frances didn't move forward, but she didn't shift away; Henry's finger began tracing small circles at the edge of her crossed thighs. Frances thought that was funny, that people are funny like that, once they have seen something, they always want to see it again. So when he turned to look at her, she laughed. He looked embarrassed so she said, don't worry, Henry. Everyone was sitting around the table talking and drinking. It's all right, she told him. She uncrossed her legs and slid toward his tracing fingers.

Denise walks from the diving board, and sits down beside her on the bench, which Frances now happens to be paying a great deal of attention to: it is made of dark brown wood; the wood is old and worn with long cracks running through it; the kind of wood you might find in the stands of local baseball parks, or smaller train stations, or beach town boardwalks; looking at it makes Frances feel happy, like she is a child again, at the beach, or walking along railway tracks in summer. She pulls up a sliver for something to do. Holds it to her nose and smells deep. It smells like wood. This night, she thinks, is just full of surprises.

Denise asks for a cigarette, which Frances lights for her, because her hands are still wet. They sit there smoking and not saying anything. Frances is grateful that Denise does not mention what they both know is happening. And grateful that when that doesn't seem to be working any longer Denise begins, so the other day at work George, you remember George, older guy, comes in everyday, funny hair, and has that thing, with his teeth . . .

– I think so, says Frances, orders the steak sandwich with fries?

– That's the one, goes Denise, so anyway, George is sitting in his seat, finishing his meal, and I put his check down beside his plate, but instead of picking it up, he does this little thing with his hand, like he wants me to lean closer. So I lean closer, and then he does this little secret look thing, back and forth, like he will be disclosing some important, sensitive piece of information. And I think to myself, Oh, isn't this nice, older man gives young girl advice on life or something like that. So I am leaning on the counter and George says very serious, I usually tip more to the girls who show a little more skin, and then he says, I tell this to you as a businessman, purely within the confines of our business relationship.

– No.

– Yes.

– So what did you do?

– I asked him how much he'd tip if I fingered myself. And then he acts all offended, like I'm the bitch. Can you believe that?

– Actually, I have absolutely no problem believing that.

– Yeah, me neither, and they laugh. And Frances thinks that it is nice to have something to laugh about; nice that Denise told her a story; nice she doesn't mention what is happening. People don't say it much these days, but it is still nice to be nice. She lights another cigarette and offers Denise one, which, her fingers now dry, she lights for herself. Then she puts her hand on Frances's arm says, oh shit, and points towards a man who is approaching quickly across the grass. He is a fat man in a striped bathrobe with a baseball bat. Underneath the bathrobe he is wearing an undershirt and a pair of baggy beige pants. His belt is undone. He is waving the baseball bat in his hand like it is a rolled newspaper.

The fat man smacks the side of the cabana with the bat and yells, what the fuck is going on here? Of course, no one answers. They all jump out of the pool and start gathering up their clothes as quickly as they can. The boys keep their eyes on the fat man, watching his bat. The fat man's eyes are busy too, staring at the breasts and asses glistening under the moonlight. It's all very quiet, just the sounds of bare feet scuffling on the ground. At the other side of the pool Frances can see Henry standing beside the girl. The others are spread out, clumsy, drunk hands trying to pull jeans on over wet skin. The fat man is staring at Denise's behind as she tries to tug her pants over it. C'mon Goddmanit, hurry it up, he says, you're lucky I don't call the cops.

– You're lucky I don't call your mother, says Ryan.

– Don't get lippy you little fuck, the fat man goes, just don't you get lippy. He gives the cabana another smack. They have to climb over a fence to get out and Frances loses sight of Henry and the girl.

They all pile into Stephen's car, but Henry and the girl aren't with them. No one says anything about it, and Frances doesn't mention it either. They drive around for a bit, and then Stephen drops her off at home and she is glad to be there. In the kitchen she makes a cup of instant coffee. She opens the back door and walks out onto the porch. It's good to sit there with her cup of coffee and a cigarette. The sky is clear. The neighbours' laundry is waving on the line. Bugs circle around the street lamp. The lamp hums low.

Frances wonders if her roommates are home. She checks John's room, then Mary's, but no luck. She decides to wait up, see if someone to comes home, see if they want to play cards. It would be fun to play cards. The coffee's given her a second wind, and there's still some beer in the refrigerator. She takes one and wanders back out on the porch. She looks up at the sky. It is clear and the stars shine bright. She puts her feet up on the rail, and tries to balance the beer bottle on her knee.

When Frances hears footsteps coming down the hall she leans her chair back and looks inside, wondering if it is John or Mary, instead she sees Henry walking down the hall and into the kitchen. Unbelievable, she says to herself. She doesn't get up or go inside. She stays out on the porch and watches him. Henry, she asks, what the fuck are you doing here?

He just stands there for a moment. Then he leans against the fridge. He pushes his baseball cap back on his head, looks up at the ceiling, and lets out a long, low sigh. Frances know this one. This one is so she will know that he is upset and thinking and feeling. She is so used to this that she lets him continue. He turns to her and says, Frances, do you have any more beer?

– Fuck you, she says and then, in the fridge. He takes one and twists the cap off. He takes a chair from the kitchen and comes out and sits on the porch.

– Henry, she asks again, what the fuck are you doing here?

– Frances, he says, I really miss you.

– Shouldn't you be missing that girl from the pool?

– C'mon Frances, he says, I really do miss you.

She can't say anything to that, so she goes inside and gets herself another beer. Stranding at the fridge she thinks, it's not as if this is the first time. It's so far past that, they are so far past the first time that she can't even get surprised, let alone angry. She looks out on the porch and sees that Henry has lit a cigarette. She goes and stands in the doorway.

– Well, what happened to her anyway? she asks.

– Oh hell Frances, he says, I don't know. I didn't fuck her if that's what you mean. I wouldn't do that. I wouldn't do that, and then come over here. You know that.

The bottle flies out of her hand and breaks near his head. He jumps out of his chair. Frances starts screaming, but even before she starts she know that these things will pass.

She pulls back the sheets. He moves gently between her legs. It is getting just light enough that she can see his face, and he is smiling. She laughs and grabs his hair, bites his lip and shoulder knowing every inch. It all comes along familiar and smooth. After, Henry turns to face the wall, and she presses her body to his. She lies quiet feeling their breathing. When she reaches her hand around he kisses her arm. Her chin is against his shoulder and her lips are just below his ear. The chlorine on his skin smells strong and new.

BALTIMORE
Cecil's

The old man who turns out to be thirty-one just last week sips on a
Coke, moves a nickel back and forth through his fingers like a fish on
a long, long trip upstream, and takes a long, long time to tell me about
his long, long habit, and all the people that died, and all the rehabs,
and all the methadone that all the nurses are cutting with something
for some reason, and he tells it all the way a normal person would talk
about all their time at medical school, and doesn't it always feel like
they want you to say congratulations, you were able to get hooked on
the most addictive drug know to man, way to go, high-five dude! I buy
him another Coke instead. Back at the hotel, feeling a bit down, I stop
by Chuck's room. He's laid out on his bed watching late-night TV. I
flop down on the other and join in. It's the usual lawyers talking about
the president's haircut, actors about their important new movies, fat
girls calling bad acne boys bitch . . . I'm half asleep, dreaming who
knows what when Chuck says, Human dignity. What? What? I say
sitting up, rubbing my eyes. Human dignity and self-respect, he
answers, in any disaster it's the first thing to go. I think that over for
a minute. Do you mean this band, or society in general? Both, he says.
Great, thanks for the pep talk, and on that cheerful note I head back
to my room. Tim is out someplace, so I smoke pot, flip on the porno,
beat off to inflated sex mutants stuffing each other with rocket-size dil-
does. In the bathroom I foolishly use the hot water and it bakes the
cum onto my hands, under my fingernails, and so I'm scrubbing away,

sweating, swearing, stoned, when I catch a glimpse of myself in the mirror . . . and it occurs to me that Chuck just might have a point.

THE PUNK ROCK SHOW pt. 172

Stephen picks Ryan up in his mom's old station wagon. They get Henry then go park behind the donut shop. *Sabbath Bloody Sabbath* is in the tape deck and they sit there listening to that, talking about how excited they are to see the Black Flag, drinking the beer, smoking the pot. They skate for a bit. Hank shows a new trick. Stephen and Ryan trying to get it . . . trying trying trying . . . when all of a sudden Stephen looks at his watch and says, Holy fuck, we're going to miss the show!

The club is packed. The band is already on. It's about eighty degrees outside and about one hundred and eighty inside. There is sweat dripping from the ceiling. Coming down the walls. Covering the floors. Sweaty girls stand at the edge of the pit. Sweaty boys stripped to the waist dive in and out of an ocean of pinwheeling, slamming bodies. Some are jumping off a stage that is only three feet high. The more adventurous are climbing the monitors to dive off them. On stage Henry Rollins is red faced, eyes bugging out, veins on this neck about to burst screaming, *rise above rise above rise above.* In the crowd every head and heart is racing wide open into the invisible light that is flooding their world. Henry (not Rollins, their Henry . . . Hank) is crowd surfing and as the ceiling is so low he somehow gets one of his legs trapped between two pipes. Ryan and Stephen point laugh at him just hanging there upside down right in the middle of the pit like some kind of sweaty punk rock pinata, while the kids thrash around him, and they think about fishing him down, but no not yet still a little too funny. The song ends and the sea goes calm and Henry Rollins looks at Hank and Hank looks at Henry and they are no more that five feet away and Henry Rollins says real quiet like, hey man, how's it hanging? And that is a true story, Hank tells the people for years.

BOSTON
The Rat

Instead of hanging around a shitty rock bar all afternoon listening to the assorted baseheads and petty criminals discuss their fascinating plans for the future, I opt for a little sightseeing in old Beantown. I tell the cabbie take me to the Gardens. Next stop Mecca. Let Henry go on about the Habs until the end of time. Blah blah blah most successful sports franchise in the entire history of human civilization. Blah, blah blah, the Rocket, Doug Harvey, Beliveau, LaFleur. Blah, blah, blah the Forum, the Flying Frenchmen, tradition. Give me the Bruins any day. Give me Terry O'Reilly, Stan Jonathan and Brad Park. The fighters. The grinders. That's my kind of team. That's what it is all about. But most of all it's all about Bobby Orr. I remember seeing him once, on TV, when I was a kid, Orr at the point, doing the spin-o-rama and then breaking in for yet another goal. Blond hair flying, Black and Gold, and unstoppable. Some nice old attendant lets me into the Gardens even though it's not a game day. I wander about soaking up the history. Then I turn a corner and there it is. The Picture. Bobby Orr in full flight after having scored the game winner, and the series winner, on Glenn Hall in fourth game of the 1970 Stanley Cup series. Standing there I feel a quiet kind of peace descend on me. Everything perfect for just one moment. And that's it. That's the best.

IRISH PEOPLE SUCK

They plan to meet at Toe Blake's before the game (they being Stephen, Bug, Ryan, Henry and Henry's cousin Declan, who is visiting from Ireland). Stephen arrives late, walks straight into Declan talking about the political situation. Stephen can hardly believe it, the political situation, of all fucking things. Normally they (being Stephen, Bug, Ryan and Henry) would simply point and laugh at anyone talking about the political situation, but apparently the Celtic-bonding ritual is in full effect, so they (being Bug, Ryan and Henry) let him rattle and hum along. The first thing Declan says to Stephen is, are you Protestant or Catholic?

– I'm Jewish.

– Well, are you a Protestant Jew or a Catholic Jew?

– That's funny, very funny, says Stephen out loud but to himself adds, my grandfather who spent the war in a concentration camp while you lousy bastards sat on your neutral asses would have thought that was very funny. Declan continues on half-drunk and half ignorant, but fully confident he knows the way. He tells them that the French people, like the Irish people, have been the victims of centuries of English tyranny; that the only solution is the liberation of Quebec and the emancipation of the long-suffering Quebecois people from the yoke of English oppression; that they should rise up and shake off their chains like dew. Stephen watches Ryan, Bug and Henry sit there heads nodding like cows.

– Idiots, he reminds them, we're the English.

– No yer not, interrupts Declan, yer Jews an' Irish. Yer the French's comrades-in-arms in their struggle against the English.

– Yeah, echoes Henry, comrades-in-arms.

– Declan my friend, Stephen politely begins, this is the new world, and here there are actually no Jews and no Irish, no French and no English, no wars that took place five hundred years ago, no history, no destiny. People might still use those words, but they don't really mean them, because the only thing that really matters here is money, and there are really only two kinds of people, people who have money and people who don't. And if you take a look around, you will see that the French now have the money. They run the businesses. They run the government. They are the power. Now I don't know much about Ireland, but what we actually have here is a small group of very ambitious people trying to get crowned king of their very own little country. What we have is a little band of little Napoleons. The rest of us are just trying to make a living in the mess they have left us.

– Typical ahistorical revisionist mentality, says Declan.

– Oh shut up, Stephen tells him and then for good measure, you deluded dickhead.

Declan jumps up yelling, take that back you prick! Take it back or I'll make you eat those focking words you skinny little focking prick.

OK, OK, easy, I take it back, says Stephen while thinking, yeah, but what else am I going to do? The guy is from a fucking war zone. He could probably kill me in a second. Shoot me in the kneecaps, break my leg bones, suck out the marrow.

Come on, we're all friends here, says Ryan and he puts his hand on Declan's shoulder. He didn't mean it, Henry says to his cousin. Let's have another round . . . on me, says Bug. Calmer heads and the promise of free alcohol prevail, and soon enough they are drinking, talking, giving Bug a hard time for being a Bruins fan, and eating mushrooms from the bag that Ryan passes around.

Out on St. Catherine's Street they make their way through the Saturday night crowds to the Forum. Stephen looks at her rising up from the corner of Atwater and St. Catherine's . . . The Montreal Forum . . . the last place of glory in our sad little city. Walking through the old halls is like returning to a land where, for a second, Stephen can almost believe his city hasn't been turned into a ghost town. For just a moment he's back on the Main with Duddy, playing dice, looking up girl's skirts, going for sandwiches at Schwartz's. They climb some stairs. Stephen is wandering from bar to coffee house, alone with Leonard, waving so long. They turn down a corridor, walk through a gateway, and out into it. Below them the ice glistens like a field of fresh diamonds. The rows of seats fan back from the ice in reds, whites then blues. And those seats are packed with the French and the English, the black and white, red, brown, and yellow, the young and old, rich and poor, men, women, boys and girls. The air is filled with the whirl of the organ, the screech of air horns, and the thunder of thousands of voices. It is thick with the smell of beer and ice and decades of victory. Stephen looks out on all the people, and the banners hanging down from the rafters, and quietly mourns. We could have been something. Instead we're just one more shit town filled with whining losers. The dynasties are all gone. The winners have left. Hang a For Rent sign over the place and the last one out turn off the lights. So be it. That's Montreal's future not mine. First chance, I'm getting the hell out of this morgue . . . just then Ryan interrupts Stephen's happy thoughts, wrapping an arm around his shoulder, all drunk smiles and says, this is going to be great! It looks like he needs to believe that, so Stephen laughs, nods back, and wraps his arm around Ryan's shoulder in agreement. Oh yeah, yells Ryan, this is going to be fucking excellent!

To Stephen's surprise, he is almost right. Both teams come out hard. It's end-to-end play. Bruising in the corners. Mad scrambles in front of the net. Desperate gambits. Brilliant saves. The organ music swells to a crescendo, pulling the crowd to its feet. Then the Bruins score. Silence. Followed by a deafening booing chorus. Bug is grinning big, so Henry punches him. But a little Boston luck can't get them down. Not now, because halfway into the period the mushrooms have locked in strong. Little lights glimmer in the corners. The walls pulse and breathe. If they get tired of the action on the ice all they have to do is look around at the crowd, who are like TV, only so much better. In the next section there is a big, fat kid with a Bruins jersey and hat. He has an air horn and a big sign: BRUINS ALL THE WAY IN 88. Whenever they get really bored, they yell out, calling him a fat fuck, and he takes a moment off from eating his hotdog, or waving his sign, to give them the finger. Henry screams at the top of his lungs: YOU DON'T EVEN UNDERSTAND THE GAME YOU FUCKING AMERICAN FUCKING GAY FUCKING FAGGOT!

Declan is sitting beside him, a little quiet, which seems odd to Stephen, who thought this kind of thing would have been right up his alley, singing songs, chanting empty slogans, random threats, the promise of group violence. Stephen asks if he's enjoying the game. Jaesus, comes the reply, I'm too focking high Stevie, the adverts . . . I cannot focking read'em. Stephen tells him they are all in French, and that calms him somewhat. But it makes Stephen wonder if they even have mushrooms in Ireland. Have you ever tripped before, he asks. Oh saure, loads of times, comes the answer. But Stephen is not so convinced and decides to keep an eye on him, in the name of improving international relations and promoting religious understanding. The Habs score two quick ones just before the end of the period. Henry is on his feet saying: Yes! Thank you God! Yes! In your face Bug, you Bruins loving faggot traitor! Then the buzzer sounds and they pile out to smoke as many cigarettes as possible during the intermission.

Declan comes alive during the second, cheering Montreal on, calling Boston a bunch of stupid cunts. Stephen starts to warm up to him, and after the third Montreal goal they celebrate with their arms around each other's shoulders. The period ends with the Habs up 3-2. During the second intermission they find themselves side by side at the urinals. Ahh yer a good one Stevie, says Declan. If only grandfather could see me now, thinks Stephen, arm in arm, down the Forum halls, with a drunken anti-Semite . . . happy happy times. But here, on this earth, happiness never lasts. Tragedy strikes in the third. Five minutes left, Partick Roy is injured after Mike Milbury runs him in the crease. Chris Chelios steps in and pummels Milbury, but both players are ejected. In seconds, they (being Stephen, Ryan, Henry, Bug, Declan, the Montreal Canadiens, their myriad legions of fans, and all other forces of good in the universe) lose their goalie and best defenceman. They (same as above) feel a shift in the night as the world slides toward evil, and sure enough it happens. They (again, same) watch helplessly as Boston scores two unanswered goals. The final tally is 4-3 Bruins. Quietly, the faithful leave the temple.

Out on the street Stephen watches reality flicker. People move all around. The world is light and sound. Bug is diplomatically concealing his delight at the Boston win. Henry is pretending it didn't happen, that it was all just some terrible nightmare. He is putting his faith in action, in movement, saying they should take Declan to Super Sexe, show him some real Montreal entertainment. Bug is in. Ryan is in. Stephen? Sure, why not, strong psychedelic drugs and soulless sexual gymnastics, it's like a horse and carriage. They turn to Declan who stands nearby looking out into the traffic with glazed eyes. Do you want to go to the ballet? Henry asks. Sounds magic mate, says Declan with a quick smile and a shake of his head, like he is waking from a dream.

At the corner of Tupper who do they see but the tubby Bruins' fan wobbling in their direction. Tubby sees them too, and as he passes by chuckles in a thick Bostonian drawl, enjoy the game, fellas? Stephen watches it unfold as certainly as spring. Henry calls Tubby a cocksucker. Tubby calls Henry a dickhead. Henry pushes Tubby. Tubby pushes Henry back. Here comes flying Declan to deliver a head-butt on Tubby, who stumbles back for a moment, like an elephant struck by a baseball bat, then recovers and punches Declan somewhere near the face. And so it really begins. Bug, Ryan and Stephen stand back as Henry, Declan and Tubby go. Tubby holds his own for a moment, but almost immediately the uneven tide turns against him. Things get very ugly very quickly and Henry steps back saying, that's enough. But not for Declan who keeps right on pummeling. Of course a crowd has formed, always interested to see just how dumb human beings can be. And they have certainly come to the right place, thinks Stephen, because dumb is what we do best. Ever since we were kids we've wrapped ourselves up in stupid, used it as a vaccine against a stupider world. TV shows, car ads, political frat parties, celebrity marriages, blowing up babies to keep oil cheap . . . you think that stuff is dumb? . . . that's nothing . . . we'll show you something that is absolutely retarded, and we'll call it our lives. Standing on the corner, strung higher than kites, all these things seem very clear, and they occur to Stephen in the time it takes Declan to kick Tubby once more. Before the next, Henry steps in to pull him back. With barely a glance, Declan turns and punches Henry, then gives Tubby another. Henry, bleeding from the corner of his mouth, smacks Declan in the side of the head, and the two start swinging wildly, tearing off bits of clothes, skin, hair. Ryan steps in between the battling cousins. Tubby lies beached and bloody on the sidewalk. The crowd keeps getting bigger. The lights are flashing. A siren blasts. Stephen looks up Tupper. The street is empty. All he needs to do is turn, put one foot in front of the other, but instead he takes hold of Henry while Ryan and Bug wrestle Declan. Henry struggles. Declan gets loose. His left comes looping. Henry ducks, and that left cracks Stephen hard in the nose.

Glasses break and fall to the sidewalk. Sparks behind the eyes. Blood dripping down the lip. And Declan hugging him, in tears, Oh Jaesus Stevie boy, I'm so focking sorry. I dinna mean to hit you, I'm so focking sorry, mate.

NEW JERSEY
Day Off

Day off, and we can really use it. Instead of making for the city, we head to New Jersey, to this little town called Point Pleasant. It's Tim's idea, says he was there when he was a kid and it's great, they've got a beach, a board-walk, mini-putt, everything. On the way we drive by this big sign for Asbury Park, and we all have to get out get our pictures taken in front of it, just like Mr. Springsteen. Finally make it to Point Pleasant and it's just as Bruce promised: Sandy, Spanish Johnny, Puerto Rican Jane and the Magic Rat. The boardwalk. Girls with makeup on. Dudes with shirts off. Cotton candy and cigarettes. The tilt-a-whirl. The ocean. Even though it's a little chilly we all go in. Then sit on the beach watching the sun go down, and no one saying much, but this time because it feels too good to talk.

BUG LEARNS TO FLY

They were all surprised when Bug got a job, and not a bad gig at that, roadie-ing for this mildly famous local band. They actually pay him, and he gets to travel to far-off towns, drink different brands of beer, meet new people and try to have sex with them. Good for the friends of Bug too, because now the shows are free. Tonight's is one of the best Ryan has seen them play, and not only because of Bug's beer tickets, which allow the taps to flow all night long. The band does kick some major ass, and the elusive smell of awesome mingles with beer, smoke and stale vomit in the nightclub air. After the show, waiting in the tiny dressing room, the singer Phil seems, once again, to Ryan, like a total asshole; bass-player Sara is nice, and very cute, the punk rock pin-up girl of every boy's dream; Chuck the guitar player is a good one, straight-edge though, so a bit of a puzzle; however, drummer Tim is just right – lazy, drunk, bored, etc. – and makes for a wonderful fit. When Tim and Bug are done, it's out into the snow, off into the bars.

First stop the Pub. Ryan recalls when it used to be frequented exclusively by old gay men and young kids with green hair. The punks liked the cheap beer, and that they were allowed in, while the elderly fags liked the kids because their dyed mops livened up the joint. Sadly, it's now become home to more drunk jocks than you can shake a stick at, and as aging queers and intoxicated football players just do not mix, the low rent Quentin Crisps have floated away leaving behind a fat sea of frat pricks. But the beer is cheap and with the drunk jocks you get the cute college girls, so they still keep coming.

They find a table and it's pitchers of draft and shots of Jägermeister for all forever. Tim and Bug tell the funny tour stories. One about Tim screwing a very large girl in Austin on the fire escape of the motel, and the swinging of the ladder, and the catching of a very bad case of Texas gonorrhea. Another concerning Bug getting arrested in Georgia for shoplifting grape juice. Thought it was wine. The only reason he's not still there is the judge assumed he was slightly retarded, felt sorry and turned him loose.

Henry soon latches onto some girls at the next table. One has big blonde hair and tits and it turns out she is the stewardess. The other has a short brown bob, a nice smile and turns out she is the friend. After seconds of idle banter the girls join them. Henry is on the stewardess like flies on sherbet. Poor Frances, thinks Ryan, don't know why she puts up with it, but I guess that's love for you, or something . . .

Soon enough it's time to go. Henry tries to convince them to stay, but for Ryan, Bug and Tim there is no way. It's time to get away from the inflato football losers and their barbie doll concubines. Time for the Bar. The stewardess wants to come but they are waiting for another friend. Henry explains the directions a good ten times, draws a map, then has an intimate *tete*-a-*tete* where promises are exchanged, and, finally, they are on their way. A short cab ride later, the entire duration of which Henry reminisces about the stewardess' chest, they are pushing open the old doors of the Bar, their home away from home. All their favourite waitresses are working. The Heinekens are flowing.

Soon enough they are on the pool tables. Making the big shots. Sending their enemies running back home to their mothers. A couple of small packets are purchased from the tall, smiling gentleman who lives by the pinball machine, and then the pool is even sharper. The beer tastes sweeter. Jokes are funnier. Cigarettes more delicious. The DJ lets the whole second side of the Replacements' *Let It Be* play. Oh yes my friends, thinks Ryan, we are Princes in our City.

By closing time they are fully polluted but still going strong. The lights come up. The crowd mills about doing the three o'clock shuffle, trying to find a party, a cigarette, a last minute late night last anything. The boys huddle figuring the next move. Tim and Bug are in, but Henry just sits moping, dreaming of blonde stewardess tits that got away, letting them know: Christy Canyon, she was pure Christy Canyon, I never saw tits like that before, never, and I could have had'em if we had stayed, but no, we had to go, I missed them because of you, all because of you . . . Boo hoo boo hoo, says Bug, here's the hand cream, now go to the bathroom, and get over it. But then in she walks and Henry's eyes pop open like the weasel's. And she's got the two friends in tow so everyone is pretty pleased.

They end up in a pair of cabs heading back to Bug's place. Ryan looks out the window. Lovely snow still falling on the city. Whiteness everywhere. Seems it's been coming down for weeks. In his cab there is Tim and the two friends. Bug slow off the mark got stuck in the other cab riding up front while Henry and the stewardess bond in back; there is no way Henry will be letting her out of his sight for the rest of the night. Ryan and Tim take advantage of the cab ride to lay some foundation with the friends.

Bug's roommate Wreck is passed out drunk on the couch, untouched pizza on the coffee table, unlit marijuana cigarette in hand, and the Hüsker Dü skipping on the stereo. His real name is Rick, but they call him Wreck on account of this kind of thing. Beers appear, and Wreck's pot is smoked and pizza eaten, still hot. Jokes are made and new records put on. More beer. The whole time Wreck snores peacefully in his chair. Ryan's friend gets sick and spends half an hour huddled around the toilet. Then she goes to sleep on the bathroom floor like a baby. Tim swoops his hardier friend off to a bedroom. Then Henry and the stewardess disappear to another. This leaves Bug and Ryan lonely together in the living room. They talk a bit more, a few more ha ha happy tour stories. Smoke a bit more pot. Listen to a few more records. Drink more beer. But behind it all is the stewardess. Like they do in the videos, she begins with little gasps, then moves to deep throaty groans, before locking in on a chant of yes, yes, yes, YES, YES, YES. Bug and Ryan give up any pretense at conversation and sit back with their cigarettes and listen. But when she starts with the fuck me, fuck me, FUCK ME HAARRRDER YOU BASTARD, Bug gets up and starts to pace the room. She's right, he says, he is a bastard.

– Tell me about it, says Ryan.

– In there with that total babe while I'm stuck out here with you.

– I know just how you feel.

– I wish I was in there.

– Me too.

– I've got to get in there.

– Yeah.

– No, I'm serious. I *have* to get in there.

– Bring back some polaroids, Ryan tells him. Bug goes over to the window. He stares out at the snow. Ryan looks over at Wreck still dead to the world. Bug turns back, that's it! he says, I've got it!

Ryan goes to Henry's room. He stands at the door for a minute. On the other side the performance is still in full swing. YES NO YES YES THERE YES THERE NOW HARD HARD HARDER. He knocks on the door. No response. He knocks again. Then pounds. The vocals stop. A moment of silence. Henry asks, yeah?

– Hank, need to talk with you.

– No, you don't.

– Yes, I do. Matter of life and death, in fact.

Henry comes to the door nude, but for the condom on his cock. This better be good, he says.

– I'm worried about Wreck.

– Everybody's worried about Wreck.

– No, right now worried. He's breathing funny.

– Are you fucking kidding?

– No, actually, I'm fucking worried, like I said.

– Where's Bug.

– Oh, he went out.

– Out?

– Yeah.

– I can't believe this. Henry takes a towel from the door and wraps it around his waist. I can't believe this, he mentions again as he follows Ryan into the living room. They stand there looking at Wreck. See, says Ryan.

– See what? That's how he always looks.

– No, Ryan tells him, this is different. Henry leans over to shake Wreck awake, when all of a sudden there is a scream from down the hall, and then another noise. Ryan follows Henry back to the room. The stewardess is by the window, butt-naked, her hands in the air. There was a man, a man at the window, she says. They look at the window. It is open. The wind blows the curtains in. Snowflakes come floating.

– Where is he now? Ryan asks.

– I pushed him, she says.

– Oh shit, Ryan races to the window, sticks his head out. And there is Bug, two floors down, lying on the sidewalk. Henry joins Ryan out the window. What the fuck? he asks.

Down on the street everything is quiet and white. Bug lies in a pile of snow in front of the bagel store. Don't move him, says the stewardess, you're not supposed to move him. She is wearing flannel pajama bottoms and Wreck's parka. No, I won't move him, says Henry shivering in an overcoat, boots and nothing else, I'll fucking kill him.

– Jesus Hank, he could be hurt, Ryan says.

– He's not fucking hurt. He bounced off the awning and fell into a pile of snow. See, says Henry pointing at the building charting Bug's descent. It's only two floors. Me and him did it last week. Now get up you fucking faker, he says to Bug.

– My legs, says Bug, I can't feel my legs.

– Bullshit, answers Henry, you get up now, or I'm going to kick the shit out of you.

– OK, maybe I can feel my legs, says Bug as he sits up, but I am kind of winded and my head hurts. The stewardess kneels down beside him and asks, are you sure you're OK? That was a pretty big fall.

– I'm OK, Bug tells her.

– I'm so sorry for pushing you. I feel so terrible. It's just that you really scared me. If I had known it was you, I wouldn't have pushed you like that.

– That's OK. It was my fault. You know, opening the window and everything. Anyone would have pushed me.

– Are you sure you're all right. Maybe you have a concussion. Maybe we should go to the hospital. She puts her hand on his head to check if he has a concussion.

– Jesus Christ, says Henry, he doesn't need to go the fucking hospital. Let's get inside. It's too fucking late for this shit.

Henry and the stewardess head back upstairs. Ryan sits down beside Bug in the snow. Fat white flakes are tumbling from the soft grey sky, covering the cars and the building, the street and the sidewalk, blanketing the trees and filling up the garbage cans. They settle down like a hundred million cotton balls, stuffing the ears of the city till the only sound is the gentle hiss of their fall.

A HIGHWAY

Back of the van

The towns and fields and the warm sun go by and I am drifting into sleep through people and places and before me in a chair at the dinner party people are well dressed and talking and the table clothe is white and the plates and the knives and forks clink clink clink so it is hard to hear the woman with the wrinkles in her neck and the blonde hair pinned up with diamonds and jewels when behind her is Gidget and we are leaving the room down a hall her hands warm and all the people and their faces line the walls Gidget squeezes come on and we are in a bathroom alone her kisses so warm and deep the clothes are falling away when the people and their faces come in through the door looking at Gidget and I so out through another room with more people more faces into a room her kisses so warm and deep the clothes come off her body like flowers her kisses so warm and deep when the people and faces come through the door so Gidget and I out the other more halls and faces and noise and people and out into the garden her kisses so warm and deep when I am awake, blinking at a service station, the van stopped, Tim pumping gas in the bright sun, everyone else in the store, and me in the back of the van, and I don't want to do anything but lie there feeling the dream of I am love.

THE SAME CROOKED WORM

Henry looked at the form: Please complete previous STD history. Next was a list of diseases with boxes beside them: If yes, please mark with an X. So he started down the list: Chlamydia: X Gonorrhea: X Syphilis: X . . . but had to stop on Genital Herpes, where it said: simplex 1 or simplex 2. Henry had genital herpes. He knew that. Those little red dots had been ruining his life since tenth grade, but no one ever said there were different kinds. Was the right answer important? Did it matter? It might matter. He went to ask the nurse. Her door was open. She was sitting at her desk, in a brown turtleneck sweater, looking at a chart. Afternoon sun filtered through orange curtains. Plants sat on bookshelves. On the walls diagrams of penises and vaginas mixed with macramé hangings. There were also two big models, one of a woman's insides and the other of a man's. They looked like The Visible Man kit Henry had when he was young, except these were the missing parts. In the kits you never got the cocks or the pussies, and Henry guessed this is where they went, because here that was all you got, in all their clear-plastic-outer, multi-coloured-interior, larger than life glory. He knocked on the frame of the open door. The nurse looked up and in a friendly but busy voice asked, Yes?

– I have a question.

– Important?

– Could be.

– Come on in, close the door, she said as she put down the chart. He sat down. She looked at him. He looked at her: Your question? she asked.

– I have genital herpes, he said.

– Yes?

– I don't know what kind.

– You mean simplex one or two?

– Yeah, that's it.

– What are your symptoms?

– I get these red dots. They last about a week. They itch.

– Where do you get them?

– On my cock, he told her. The nurse smiled. Where on your penis? she asked. Henry had to think about that one. He didn't know the exact word for the place. It wasn't on the end. It was under the knob, just to the left, what was the name for that place? He held out his index finger. If this was my cock, he told her, just about here. And he pointed to a spot below the first knuckle, an inch or so from the nail.

– On the shaft, just below the head, she said.

– Yeah that's right, he confirmed, on the shaft.

– And they are little red dots?

– Yeah.

– Do they start as clear blisters? Then pop, and leave the dots?

– Yeah, that's it exactly.

– Do you ever have any lesions?

– No, he said then asked, how do you mean? The nurse quickly leafed through a stack of pamphlets on her desk. She pulled one out, opened it up, and showed him a page with pictures on it. Do you ever have anything that looks like this? she asked. He looked at the colour photographs. Angry red sores boiled on cocks and pussies.

– No, never, never like that, he said, that must be the one I don't have.

– It's hard to tell, said the nurse, these are all cases of simplex two, which, as you can see, is usually more severe. Generally, people have simplex one in the oral areas, and simplex two is in the genital. But they can be traded back and forth, with oral sex.

– OK, said Henry.

– The bottom line is, it doesn't really matter which one you've got. Just be honest with future sexual partners, always use condoms, and if you are interested there are some expensive drugs that don't really work.

– Thanks.

– You're welcome, said the nurse. She started looking at some papers on her desk.

– Actually, I needed to know for this form, said Henry, I'm here for an AIDS test.

– Oh, said the nurse, can I have that? He passed her the form. She looked at it for a minute then said, you've been to the clinic before?

– Oh yeah.

– Just a moment, I'll go get your file. She left the room. Henry looked at the plastic models of sexual organs. It was like looking at giant bugs. It'd been that way since he'd heard. Ever since he had found out about Tammy his interest in sex had dried up like an orange in the desert. He tried to remember the last time he had even beat off. Must be more than two week ago, he told himself. Hadn't even thought about it. All he could think about was did she really have it? When did she get it? Before or after we fucked? Did he have it? How many girls had he fucked since then? How many times with Frances since then? How many with a condom? How many without? Can you get it from kissing nipples? From licking a pussy? From putting your finger in an ass? Why did I always, he asked himself, put my finger in their asses? Why did I do that? He looked at his fingers, they looked OK now, but what about then, were there little cuts? There were probably little cuts. And there were always cuts in asses, little tears; anyone with an ass knew that. A finger sliding, a tongue lapping, fluids mingling, these days that's all it took. One little moment, one little thing you liked, an idiosyncrasy really, and now it could mean your life. He thought about that. But most of all he thought why did I fuck all those girls? Why? Ever since he could remember, all his time had been spent thinking about sex. Imagining sex. Wanting sex. Looking for sex. And now that was gone. Now when he looked around at all the people he thought these people are crazy. Men looking for women. Women looking for men. Everyone looking for anyone. Pussies dripping. Asses tightening. Cocks spurting. And the tits. Everywhere the tits. Always the tits. To be squeezed. Sucked. Licked. Sex everywhere. In everything. The whole world chasing it like the Holy Grail, only better, sweeter, hotter, deeper, harder baby please right there don't stop don't you dare stop . . . and just one short week ago, Henry thinks on, I had been running with that crowd, lungs full, legs pumping to the next sex, but now I am standing by the side of the road barely watching, and all I think about is dead.

The nurse walked back in with his chart. She looked at it for a bit. Then she said, Henry, a lot of people with histories similar to yours are worried about HIV and AIDS, but unless you have been involved in high risk activity, there is no real need for testing.

    – I had sex with a girl who has it and I didn't use a condom.

    – Right, well that fits into the high-risk category, tell me all about it. So Henry told her all about Jimmy, bit of a junkie, who had it; told her about the girls who slept with Jimmy who now had it; told her that one of them was Tammy; told her how people asked, did you sleep with her? Or him? Or her? And people said, no, not me, never. But alone they all remembered who, and when, and if they had used a condom, done it more than once, or in the ass, or sucked a cock, licked a pussy, etcetera. Henry remembered it all very clearly: Tammy without a condom, no oral, no anal, but he did put his finger in her ass. He told the nurse all about it.

(two weeks later)

Henry knew where the telephone was. It was in the living room, on the table, in front of the TV. It was black. Old fashion. You had to dial the numbers. He walked in (again) and sat down on the couch. He stared at the phone. Somewhere a person was waiting to give him the news. All he had to do was call and read off this number: 7142. And they would tell him: positive or negative; thumbs up, thumbs down. He stared at the phone (again). The receiver was heavy and cold. He started to dial. He thought,

I'm just dialing numbers. Not a big deal. Just a few numbers. From the other end he heard a ring (again). He told himself, It's just a sound. No big thing. There was another ring, and then suddenly a young woman said, good afternoon, your number please. Last time it had rung seven times. The time before eight or nine, maybe even more. Many rings. Many. Not twice. Never just twice. While Henry was thinking about this he heard his voice say: 7142. Please hold, she said. Then she was gone. So Henry held. But his hand began trying to pull the phone away from his ear. He wanted to hang up. He wanted to hold on. A see-saw of the mind. Up or down. Up or down. Up down up down up down up . . . and she was back. Before he could say hold on a second, let's talk about this a bit, she said, your test result for the HIV virus is negative. Negative? Yes, negative, have a nice day. Then she was gone (again). Henry was alone, holding the empty telephone. A nice day? He looked around. The room was exactly the same. Except it was perfect. Invisible waves of perfect were rolling across perfect everything. They came in surges, and a bit like acid, just when you think it is done . . . whooaa my friend, there it is, back again. Henry sat down on the couch. He stretched out, stared at the ceiling, listened to the cars pass by outside, soaked in the perfect life pumping through the chairs and the rug and the TV. He had imagined that if it wasn't him, if he didn't have it, that he would run down the street laughing, kiss strangers, that he would dance, jump and shout. But now all he wanted was to lie on the couch and feel the perfect world living all over him.

Tammy had never called. They had never talked about it. Henry wondered what she'd thought about it, if she had looked at her calendar and thought that he was OK, or if the whole thing was too much, and she just couldn't call, couldn't do anything like that. I could understand that, he thought, I'd have probably done the same. But you just couldn't tell with other people. You could guess, but you were never really going to know. That's how this life was. You meet people, you do things together, then they fall away like little fireworks into the night, there is a tiny aftertaste that lingers on, but all you ever really know is the one small thing that happened, that one burst of shared light, and everything else is a guess.

On the couch Henry thought about phoning her, but what would he say, Hi, just calling to let you know I'm OK. And after that what, sorry you're not . . . but don't worry . . . everything is going to be all right . . . you'll see . . . so he didn't call. Instead he kept thinking about her. They'd only been together that one time. It was one of those lonely weeknights no one wants to go out on, no one is around, and you wander the empty town looking for that other empty someone. Henry walked through a door and saw her sitting alone at the bar. They didn't know each other well, just well enough for him to go over and say hello. They shared a drink, a laugh, a few stories, more drinks, then a walk back to her place, some crummy punk rock flop in an abandoned warehouse. She lit the candles that sat on her floor, on her windowsill, on her milk-crate bookshelves, and a stick of incense. Billie Holiday sang from a tape deck on her desk, the only real piece of furniture in the room, other than her futon. They smoked hash and talked about families and friends, her boyfriend, Henry's girlfriend, her hometown, records they liked, movies, things that had happened when they were kids, and all those other topics almost perfect strangers cover before taking off their clothes.

Through the sheet of plastic stapled over the window Henry could see the snow falling in the early morning light. He watched Tammy unbutton her shirt. Her hair was so blonde it was almost white, her breasts larger than they had looked under flannel. He kissed her neck and shoulders, down soft skin to hard nipples. Panties slid off to reveal a blonde pussy. So blonde it was almost white. Henry had never seen a pussy like that before and he stared. She giggled, you like my pussy? Oh yeah, I like your pussy. He pressed his face up against her. He remembers she smelled fresh, like hay, or soap. More kissing. More touching. Then his naked cock was sliding inside her. Slipping hot and wet. They just kept kissing and slipping into each other. For the longest time it went on, the slipping in and sliding out. He remembers they were glowing and didn't ever want to stop. Then she whispered, I like it from behind. He remembers her looking over her shoulder, everything else spread open, and her eyes so sweet and smiling, hurry up . . . put it back in . . . my pussy's getting lonely. He had never heard a girl talk like that, say my pussy's lonely. It sounded so soft on his ears, like the fresh snow outside. He put his cock in her pussy, his finger in her ass. On the couch Henry remembers that it kept on and on the sliding in and slipping out, and how she must have felt him getting close, because she pulled away and had him lie on his back. Gently she lowered herself down. Made a little sound as her pussy gripped his cock like a hand. Slowly and firmly, with the smile of a person happy and perfectly at home in their work, she stroked. And when he was done, she leaned her lips down to his ear and said so quiet, did you have a good cum? On the couch Henry remembers her voice, did you have a good cum? On the couch he remembers her warm breath as she whispered in his ear, her nipples brushing over his chest, her pussy on his cock, her warm voice. On the couch Henry gives one last pull and it all comes rushing back . . . Tammy, Oh Tammy . . .

NEW YORK CITY
CBGB's

Two shows today. This afternoon the all ages matinee show for the kiddies. Then tonight we do the same routine for the drug addicts and computer geeks. I call Stephen to tell him he is on the list, but his secretary says he is out of town, would I like to leave a message, which I do, which is: blow me. Between sets Tim and I meet two very crazy girls. After a few drinks they drag us out of the club, to under the stairs of the next building, and we are pretty much side by side, fucking these two crazy girls; Tim and I could hold hands if we wanted, though of course we don't. That night's show is real good for a change. The crowd is fair-sized. Maybe even two hundred. The band hits the stage running. Phil and Sara and Chuck jumping up and down Tim pounding on his kit. The sniffling hipsters nod their heads, which sort of counts for something. After it's done Tim and I and a few others sit at the bar. I keep thinking of Gidget. The drunker I get the more I think about her, and about the girls that afternoon, and about the difference there, and soon I am telling him all about that. Tim, I'm telling him, don't you ever get tired, feel worn out, with fun, that it's too much fun, because after too much fun, fun stops being fun. You know? Sure, says Tim, of course, and then lays a big line on the table.

PUNK'S PROGRESS

Ryan and Henry are working at Henry's uncle Terry's sweatsuit factory; but it's not just sweatsuits, they also do t-shirts, shorts, all types of sportswear; however, they don't really make the clothes there on the premises, the real work is farmed out to old women who sew at home, the factory actually just a warehouse, one room big as a football field, where shelves lined with boxes of sports clothing dyed all the colours of the rainbow tower like apartment blocks. Terry became the owner of the sweatsuit factory after his friend Timmy, the original proprietor, went to jail for something to do with racing horses, and Iranians, and heroin, and breaking the law.

After Ryan dropped out of university Henry got him the job. The work is dumb, folding clothes and pulling orders. The money's not great, but then, reasons Ryan, what can you expect for performing tasks they could probably train a monkey to do faster stronger better. The one good part is there are few hassles. If you don't show up, it's no real problem. And when too tired, too hung-over you simply climb up onto the shelves, hide in a box, pull a sweatshirt over your sleepy hurting head and drift to the land of nod.

Some afternoons when work is done, usually a Friday, Terry takes them to Nittollo's Bar & Grill on the St. Jauques strip. They drive over in his white Cadillac then sit at the bar, on red vinyl seats, in the five p.m. darkness, and listen to Terry's stories of playing semi-pro hockey in Dallas, in Oshawa, in Kansas City; of all his friends and all the crazy things they did when they were young; of Montreal in the good old days before the politicians fucked it up. All the while regulars drift in, aging tough guys with exotic dancing girlfriends, younger hoodlums with chips perched on their shoulders, factory workers and lonely receptionists, taxi drivers and dollar store clerks, and all the other assorted barflys, and they all say their hellos and take their places. Outside the sun goes down on the strip, but the lights of the bars and restaurants and motels shine on in the night.

However, this Friday is different. This Friday it's good-bye to Stephen and Bug. So first they are going out for dinner, then the Bar, then a party at Bug's apartment. Bug is going on tour and Stephen is leaving for school in California. Henry says it is good-bye for Frances as well. She's just going to McGill, Ryan tells him, just moving up to the Plateau. Might as well be Europe, predicts Henry.

As the sweatshirts are folded, Ryan thinks about all this leaving, but mostly about Stephen's heading west young man, and he thinks you can't blame him. He's got the right idea. You have to get out of this place. You can't stay here. Most people think politics is a joke, but it's not so funny when they wreck your hometown, and you can't live there anymore, unless you want to work in a sweatsuit factory, folding t-shirts for $5.35 an hour; no, that's not really all that funny. Ryan folds another shirt and keeps thinking about Stephen thinks we're not as close as we used to be, but he's still my best friend. That kind of thing doesn't change. Tonight we'll probably end up sitting out back of the Bar, in the alley, talking about our lives, our hopes for the future, our plans. And I have all kinds of plans. I've got things

I'm going to do. Lots of things. Big things. The same as Stephen. Later we'll probably walk along the dark streets, go for a late night snack at the Main, just like old times. Then stand at the corner, under a streetlight, and wish each other luck as we set out on our new lives, friends forever, apart but together, walking into all of our bright new tomorrows.

Dinner is at a Thai restaurant. Bug and Frances are already there, sitting at a table, snacking on shrimp crackers and ice-cold Singha beers. Henry and Ryan sit down. Where's Stephen? asks Ryan. Said he might be late, answers Frances. They order more Singhas. Henry starts telling a story about work: The Story of Terry's Mug and Young Kevin. Terry had a mug. A gift. One of the salesmen had visited Ireland and brought it back for him. And it was a beautiful thing to behold, tall and green and covered with shamrocks and shillelaghs. And oh how Terry loved that mug. He would walk back into the warehouse, sipping his morning coffee, and say, hey boys, have you seen this mug?

– Yes Terry, they would answer.

– It's beautiful, just beautiful when someone brings you a gift, isn't it?

– Yes Terry.

– What did you boys get me last time you went away?

– Nothing Terry. And on and on it would go. Until the day Kevin met the mug. Kevin being a kid, who was, like the mug, from Ireland, and some friend of a some cousin of some friend, and given a job for those very reasons. Early one morning he knocked the mug off the table. It shattered on the concrete floor.

He looked at it. He looked around. The coast seemed clear. Moving quickly, he set about putting the mug back together again, finding each little piece, binding them with packing tape, till it looked like a sickly lump of plastic; though, to be fair, behind the folds of clear tape little cracked shamrocks could still be seen. Stealthy Kevin put the mug back in the office kitchen, and then went on his way, his escape clean and shiny. Except that Henry and Ryan had witnessed the whole tragic thing.

An hour later, the call came down from the office that there was going to be a meeting. The entire staff, the salesmen, the secretaries, and the working boys gathered around Terry, who stood in the middle of the warehouse. In his hand was the mug. Sometimes you receive a gift, said Terry barely holding back the tears, that really means something. To others it is just a key-chain, a tie, or, maybe, a simple mug from the land where your dear mother was born . . . but to you, it is everything. And then, sometimes, some selfish bastard sneaks up and steals it all away from you. Just like that. And sometimes, the gutless prick doesn't even have the balls to own up! They just wreck your dreams and disappear, like a thief in the fucking night!!

Then Terry held up the mug for everyone to see. LOOK AT THIS! he screamed, THIS IS BULLSHIT! He threw the mug to the cement floor where it shattered, again, as best it could, wrapped in plastic, at the feet of Kevin, the Irish kid. It was very quiet in the warehouse. No one said a word. Then Kevin sniffled, Ah'm so focking sorry Terry. Ah broke yaer moog. Tears brimmed in the kid's eyes. It got even quieter. Then Terry said, Jesus fucking Christ, look at the kid's face! Jesus son, it's a joke . . . a fucking joke! . . . and everyone burst into whales of laugher. It flooded the warehouse. Up and down the aisles in waves. So fucking funny I almost vomited, tells Henry as he pours another glass of beer. Ha ha ha, Ryan agrees, and it just gets better every time I hear it. Then the waiter arrives. Well maybe no Stephen, says Frances, we might as well order.

At the Bar they drink alcohol and smoke cigarettes. They sit at tables. Go to the bathroom. The DJ plays their favourite songs. They shoot pool. The bathroom. They drink more and smoke more. Play pinball. Ryan looks around and sees that he will fold sweatshirts sit in this Bar till the day he dies. Ryan sees that his town will bury him. Henry leans over, I can't believe that dick didn't even show up to his own going away party, what a fucking asshole. But Ryan's not surprised. Stephen was a winner. And they were losers. It was like with animals. The strong avoid the weak and the sick. They just can't stand the smell. Fuck him, says Henry, you and me are staying forever. Never giving up. We will stay in Montreal and fight! Yeah, OK, sure, Ryan tells him, sounds like fun, let's do that.

At Bug's apartment the all night late-night party is in full swing. Lampshaded heads bobbing to the music. The fridge somehow stays beer full, ashtrays overflow while the butts keep coming, spliffs roll and roll, little packets get pulled out of wallets and powders are cut into thin white beaches. Ryan looks around the room, at all his friends, Bug and Tim arm wrestling, Frances looking for a light, Henry slipping out the back, pulling along a girl with bad skin, bad hair, bad clothes, bad shoes, large breasts . . . but no Stephen.

Up on the roof there is a couch, a big armchair and an old barbecue that looks like a spaceship waiting under the stars. Ryan takes a seat on the couch and looks out at his city at night, still on its feet, one last dance before they turn on the lights, and he thinks the only thing I hate more than this fucking place is me in this fucking place. Darkness starts to run out, the sky slipping into more comfortable purples and blues, shadows crawling to their corners. Then Frances is sitting beside him on the couch, taking a drag from his cigarette. From down below the sounds of the party drift up. They watch the horizon brighten to the colour of a nosebleed. Frances opens a beer and passes it over. Then she says, so what are you going to do?

– Probably go home. It's late. I should really get some sleep.

– Shut up. You have to do something. Go back to school. Something.

– Don't worry about me. I've got plans.

– Like?

– Like plans.

– Plans?

– Yes, plans.

– What kind of plans?

– Big plans. Future plans. Big, future plans.

– OK, if you don't want to talk about it.

– That's right, agrees Ryan, I don't. Instead they smoke another cigarette. Share her beer. Then start to kiss. Her shirt fumbles open. Under his lips her nipples stiffen but she says, come on, it's too late, and we're too fucked for this kind of stuff. And again Ryan has to agree. So they button up, sit there on the couch, watch the new day rising.

NEW HAVEN
The Rainbow

Tim finds some real MDMA, which I haven't seen in years, let alone taken, apparently brewed by local student chemists, so to celebrate my new sensitivity I take three. Back at the motel there is a jittery young fellow with black-framed glasses from the college paper wanting to do an interview. OK baby, says open lovey Tim. OK, Jittery says, the problem with your band is that it's the same old thing, white bread unhappy childhood lost the girl pass me a Rolling Rock blah blah blah bullshit, I mean really, who cares about all that old junk, I mean what we need now is something fresh, something that would sound like Charles Manson painting donkeys, the Marqis de Sade on ice, needles and pins and internet Mackenzie Phillips ass sex, spaceships to Saturn, time travel Napoleon and the math of black holes, nu paradigms, nu stories, nu visions, I mean, we need nu songs that explain our nu two dimensional world, I mean, that's what we really need right now! Tim ponders this for a second then says, you are absolutely right, kisses Jittery on the mouth and wanders off. But not me, even in the glow of chemical love I have a little hate left, so I line Jittery up and ask, name one? What? One thing of value you have ever created. That's not what I'm talking about. No motherfucker, that's what I am talking about. That is exactly what I am fucking talking about, motherfucker. Later Tim and I find each other alone in my room and stay up up up up talking about girls and how much we love girls and love and how much we love the girls we love and it is all finally making so much sense until eleven or so in the morning, when we come down down down and all off a sudden all of it makes no sense at all and we lie in on the floor and want to die. Oh yeah, somewhere in there I call Gidget to explain the fascinating new insights to her answering machine. It takes seven messages. Fed-exing her some of my poo would probably have been more romantic. And successful.

THE PUNK ROCK SHOW pt. 319

Bug borrows the band's van and they all drive down to New York City to see the Replacements at the Ritz. As soon as they cross the border they stop at some gas station/beer store and buy about one thousand beers and one hundred packs of Camel lights. Walking out, hands full, Ryan and Henry both thank the good lord for cross border shopping. The whole way down it is all Mats all the time. The idea was to play the albums in order: *Stink, Sorry Ma, Hootenanny, Let It Be, Tim* and *Boink*; however, as the devil fools with even those that are best laid, this simple plan leads to a fight between Bug and Henry. It starts with Henry giving a little rock talk, claiming that *Boink* came out before *Tim* and, accordingly, that the order of the play list is off. Bug who is manning the tape-deck, and therefore responsible for said crime, rebuts, well how come if *Nowhere Is My Home* is on *Boink* and *Nowhere Is My Home* is an out-take from *Tim* that they left off the album because it sounded like crap, then how could *Boink* have come out before *Tim* if they hadn't even recorded the fucking song yet? And there it is on side two of *Boink*. So shut the fuck up, finishes Bug. Then Henry calls Bug gay. Then someone says *Boink* isn't really a real Mats album anyway, it's a compilation, so both of you are gay shut the fuck up.

With that settled the drive continues on, and they all drink more beer, but that American beer is so weak that a fellow has to drink about fifty sixty to get anywhere, and this leads to another problem. They have to stop about every other minute or so for someone to pee. And of course they got going late so time starts to be a concern, though mostly for Frances, who feels very, very strongly about Paul Westerberg. As the clock ticks she starts to lose her composure. She begins: You guys have to stop drinking. But that doesn't work so well. Then she continues: You guys have to stop peeing. Which is also a limited success. She really starts to get crazy as the sun goes down and they are still two hours from NYC so she takes the wheel and won't stop and they have to piss out the back van windows all the way down the interstate.

They walk in midway through *Colour Me Impressed* so know they're OK, because that's always the opener. Third song in Tommy drops his pants. Bob is in a dress in a mess. Paul is sing cry laughing. Chris is holding it all sort of together sort of. Ryan stands with Frances just to the left of the stage where it's warm and hazy and beautiful, and there are drinks and cigarettes, cigarettes and drinks, and the songs keep coming. They try to cover *Help Me Rhonda*, but the only way you'd know is Paul says, this one is called *Help Me Rhonda*. But when they do *Sixteen Blues* Ryan almost starts to almost cry. Then all of a sudden Henry is up there on stage dancing around. Ryan watches, figures they are going to freak out, but instead Paul offers him a sip of his beer and Henry takes a good swallow, then dives off the stage, into the crowd, just in time to avoid being pulverized by the massive bouncer. Then, for some reason, Paul tosses his guitar up in the air and plunges in after him, only to break his finger. So that's the end of the show. And that was the last time they played with the original line-up because like two weeks later they kicked Bob out of the band. And everyone knows what happened after that. So, basically, the final conclusion reached by all in the van that night: the end of the original Replacements, all Henry's fault.

POUGHKIPSIE
Chances

Basically, the whole thing is a nightmare. The promoter abandoned the gig, no PR, no press, no nothing. At eleven there are about twelve people there. The band goes out and tries their best but what are you going to do? Like someone once said, shit is shit is shit. By the time I'm done breaking down the stage everyone is gone but Tim who has joined forces with Jill, an old drug buddy of ours, and they sit pounding at the bar. I tell him the last ride home is leaving. That's OK, he slurs, very comfortable right here. Come on let's go, I try to pull him off his barstool. Let go, he says, you're not the king of me! It's a hard argument to beat. Back at the hotel, I slip into bed and a restless sleep. It doesn't last. At six thirty the phone rings. By seven I am down at the police station. The desk officer says they found Tim and a woman known to local police swerving a car the wrong way down a street frequented by crack dealers and their clientele. He shows me a copy of Tim's arrest transcript. The officer asks him to recite the alphabet. Tim begins, A . . . D . . . L . . .Q . . . Q . . . and that's where the transcript ends. On the drive to Buffalo we have to stop every half hour so Tim can puke. Team spirits are very high. Get it . . . very high.

THE STUPID AND THE CONTAGIOUS

Sitting on the counter Frances watches Henry take aim and then neatly bounce a quarter off the kitchen table into a glass. A little splash of beer rises as the quarter sinks to the bottom. Henry laughs at Bug, feeling thirsty?

– Totally, your mom's pussy left a really bad taste in my mouth.

– That's very funny . . . now drink up.

– Thank you, says Bug before he drains the glass with one gulp and cockily sets it back down. It's a good front, but everyone can see he is starting to turn a little green. Frances watches Ryan dump the quarter onto a tea-towel, then fill the glass and push it back to the middle of the table; keeps watching as Henry quickly dries the quarter and moves in for the kill; then thinks, for most amateur alcoholics and aspiring barflies quarters is a way of passing the boring, intoxicated hours, but for these boys it has become a Machiavellian contest of betrayal and intrigue. They form alliances, plot, double, even triple cross each other. Tonight Bug has been singled out because he has the unbelievable gall to be a Bruins' fan. Fingering the quarter Henry looks at him like a hyena eyeing a sickly baby gazelle.

The boys play in the kitchen because the table has that good bounce, just the right combination of elasticity and firmness that they require. Some other friends are in the next room watching the hockey, and the soothing sounds of the Lemonheads' first album that drift from the stereo are occasionally punctuated by their cheers, or groans, depending on the Habs' fortunes. The boys have a smaller TV set up in here so they won't miss the big game: Boston at Montreal. And Frances knows games don't get much bigger than that, at least not around here they don't.

Henry is just about to bounce again when Ryan cries out, MOTHERFUCKER! All eyes immediately flip from the war on the table to the war on the ice where, in flickering colour, Patrick Roy lies sprawled out, the puck sits in the net and Cam Neely raises his hands in celebration. The announcers go off in French, complaining about the treachery of referees; the boys now watch the games in French because they have come to believe that the English commentators don't love the Canadiens enough. As the rest of the Bruins crowd around Neely, Bug lights a cigarette and with a big grin says to Henry, how about that, cockface?

Henry just sneers in disgust, Cam Neely is a gay bigfoot that they shaved and trained to skate, and you're his little back-door punk . . . now get ready to drink. With that settled he turns his attention to the table. They all watch as Henry balances the quarter between his thumb and index finger. He adjusts to ensure that it hits at just the right angle. Down goes the hand. Down goes the quarter. It strikes the tabletop hard and true, flips up in a graceful arc, then plops dead center into the glass of beer. He pushes the glass toward Bug with a smile. Puke and cry, he suggests.

– Cheers, Bug answers as he lifts the glass and starts to drink, but it is slow going. His Adam's apple bobs sluggishly. A thin line of beer starts on the left side of his mouth and trickles down his chin. Behind the glass his face turns green, then grey, then a deeper green. Oh shit, there she blows, says Ryan as he rises out of his seat, anxious to put some distance between Bug and himself. Bug coughs a mouthful of beer back into the glass, showering the table with a fine mist. Wreck, Henry and Tim are safe on the other side of the table, but they push their chairs back just to be sure. The first rush of vomit goes into the glass. It sprays back onto Bug and sprinkles Ryan, who is now desperately trying to get away. His face flecked with bits of his dinner, Bug lowers the glass and turns toward the wall. Tim bravely rushes in with the bucket. All eyes are on Bug as he opens his mouth and a river of puke comes roaring out. Frances stares in awe. The boys howl with delight. Bug fills the bucket.

After it is done he rests with his elbows on his knees, his head hanging down, trying to catch his breath. Bits of sick drop to the floor. Poor Bug, says Frances.

– Holy fuck, says Wreck.

– Never seen anything like that, says Tim.

– Best puking ever, hands down, says Ryan.

– That's what you get for being a Bruins fan, concludes Henry. Tim helps Bug to the shower and the others start to conveniently wander away from the vomit-laden table. Hold on, Frances tell them, I am not cleaning this mess up.

– OK, says Henry still walking.

– You can't just leave it here.

– Jesus Frances, take a pill, we'll clean it up . . . after the game. And he disappears into the next room. Everyone else is gone, except Ryan who is standing by the fridge opening a beer. It looks like it is you and me kid, she tells him.

– I don't know, Frances, he answers, I mean you're nice and everything, but I'm not sure if I'm ready to get involved.

– Listen asshole, just get the stupid mop.

When they are done Ryan and Frances take a marijuana rest out on the kitchen fire escape. As they smoke she tells him about her program, a joint major in French Literature and Women's Studies. She tells him about working at the radio station on the Rawk Girl Rawk Hour. He laughs and asks if there are enough girl rock bands to fill a whole hour, and they get into a discussion of what a girl band is, that largely consists of Ryan repeating that Sonic Youth are 75% dude, while Frances maintains the Kim Gordon's songs still count. Sensing an impasse, she changes subjects, asks if he has heard from Stephen, and he tells about last week's postcard of Mickey Mouse with EVERYONE HERE SUCKS scrawled on the back.

They are about to go in when the apartment building backdoor screeches open. A second later two people walk out into the alley. It is too dark for them to see much except shady outlines that stop at the nearest garage, and start to kiss. Now fairly stoned, Ryan and Frances elbow one another, giggle quietly, but keep watching. The boy has the girl up against the wall and they are moving together, slowly grinding into each other, hands slip under shirt, moonlight shines on a set of hazy milk white jugs. Wow . . . nice tits, says Frances. Yeah, agrees Ryan as the boy moves between the girl's legs, but then she pushes him back. Not here, she says buttoning up. Ryan shakes his head recognizing the voice of their good old friend Denise, starts to smile, but

stops when he hears Henry say, OK, let's go back to my place.
Henry takes her hand and they stroll off down the alley. Frances
and Ryan watch till they reach the end and turn left on
Sherbrooke.

– Doesn't that freak you out? asks Ryan.

– No, she laughs, I stopped worrying about that kind of thing
a while ago. Then Frances puts her arm around his shoulder and
says, let's go see our old friend Mr. Booze.

Back inside Bug has showered, changed, and is back for
more, sitting with Tim and Wreck at the table. Ryan fixes the
drinks and Frances takes a seat. Bug is telling a tour story, so we
were in San Antonio, and after the show me Tim a couple of local
guys and girls took acid and drove out to the desert. You know,
look at the sky, the stars, the bushes, the rocks, all that stuff.
Anyhow, when we finally get back to the hotel we see a big
crowd out front. So we're sitting in the van freaking cause it's late
and we're on acid, and we're in the middle of Texas, and who the
fuck are all these people outside our hotel? Cops? CIA? Lynch
mob? We don't know. But then we notice a couple of the guys
from the road crew, and a couple of the guys from the show that
night. So we're all relieved that they're friendly and not some
band of rednecks out stringing up punk rock queers. We walk
over but I'm still kind of wondering why these guys are standing
around outside the hotel at four in the morning when this piece
of shit comes falling from the sky. And it lands like less than two
feet away from me. And we're on acid. In Texas. And there's this
piece of shit. From the sky. So I look up, and on the fourth floor
balcony, an ass is hanging over the railing. Now I don't know
these people all that well, so I ask one, excuse me, but what the

fuck are they doing? He says they are playing Plop, and that's it, like that is an answer. So I go, oh, thanks, but what the fuck is Plop? It's this game where you try to shit into a cup from a really high place, he says. I look over and see that yeah, there is this cup on the ground, and there are three or four shits lying around it. Bug finishes his story by slamming his hand against the table while proclaiming, and that's their game! They shit in a cup from a very high place! Can you fucking believe that? Like this is something so twisted that *even* he can't believe it, but thinks Frances, deep down I bet he is just jealous he didn't think of it first.

After that they have a few more drinks, tell a few more stories. Wreck falls asleep sitting-up, a favourite party trick of his. Ryan takes out his bag of weed to roll yet another, but can't find his papers. They all check pockets but no one has. The boys start to panic; Bug looks in the kitchen drawers, under the sink, in the cupboards; Ryan checks the bathroom; Tim the living room. After a few minutes of fear, Tim returns triumphant, papers in hand. Ryan starts to roll while Bug is drawing portraits on a pad of paper with a magic marker he found in one of the drawers. Soon enough the joint starts to make its way around the table.

Frances is in the bathroom when she hears a commotion start up in the kitchen. There is a lot of snickering and stifled laughter mixed with cautions to be quiet and shut the fuck up, dude. Then she hears Bug say Do it . . . Do it . . . then the laughing gets louder and louder and louder.

She walks into the kitchen. The boys are standing around Wreck, who is still asleep but now stripped to his underwear. JETHRO TULL RULES is stenciled across his chest in large black letters. Oh my God, she says and approaches for a closer look. His body is covered with pictures and words, all of it totally rude, like an obscene, adolescent version of the Illustrated Man. On Wreck's upper lip they have written the instructions: INSERT COCK HERE, and in case that's not clear enough they've included two arrows pointing to his mouth. The boys are in hysterics. All they can do is say LOOK!! LOOK!! and point at Wreck like this is the funniest thing ever; like this is all the comedies ever made concentrated into one little pill that they are rolling around on their tongues. Tim has the marker in his hand and is finishing a large I AM THE GAYLORDEST that runs elbow to wrist on Wreck's left arm. Bug is saying . . . he . . . has to . . . go to a family dinner . . . TOMORROW NIGHT!! . . . WITH HIS GRANDMOTHER!! . . . and job interview . . . first thing . . . MONDAY MORNING!! Hearing this the boys collapse on the floor in convulsions of laughter. All Frances can do is smile and shake her head.

It is morning by the time they call it a night. They leave Wreck at the table snoring peacefully, looking like a fierce but retarded Maori warrior. Ryan and Tim crash on the couch in the living room. Bug goes to his bed. Frances takes Wreck's. Waiting for sleep to come she wonders about these boys she grew up with, who don't seem to be doing much of that. Maybe it is the October chill; maybe it was seeing her old boyfriend suckle her old best friend's tits in a back alley; or maybe it's just the large amounts of drugs and alcohol she's ingested over the last twelve hours, but this night feels like an end. And as she slips into anesthetized dreams she sees herself walking along the halls of their old elementary school, but the classrooms are empty, and her footsteps echo through the deserted building. At the front door she gets onto a train that is pulling out of a station. She takes a seat by the window and there, just outside, sees her old friends sitting on a bench, waiting, but there are no more trains, and it is Sunday night, past dinnertime, and it is starting to rain.

Next morning they are all very hung-over. In the kitchen it is a coffee and cigarette breakfast. Wreck is in the shower scrubbing; he's been there for the last half hour. Tim lies like a dead thing on the couch. Bug gets up and goes to the fridge where he rummages, then comes up with a beer. He twists off the cap and takes a big sip. Then he does something Frances can't believe. She though she'd seen it all with these boys, but Bug shows her something new. He takes out his cock and starts to pee in the bottle. She is sipping her morning coffee as Bug is peeing into a beer bottle. What the fuck are you doing? asks Ryan speaking for both of them.

– This is another excellent game Tim and I learned on tour. It's called The Lottery, Bug tells them. When the bottle is full again, he twists the cap back on and puts it in the fridge. Get it? he asks.

– You should stop touring, says Ryan, it's really messing you up.

– Take the beer out of the fridge, Frances tells Bug.

– It's funny, he says.

– No, it's not funny, she tells him.

– You take it out if you want, but I'm not ruining the joke.

– Don't be an idiot, she tells him.

– Don't be an idiot, he tells her in a high-pitched voice.

– The level of this conversation is quickly sinking below demented, she tells him.

– The level of this . . . Bug begins. She is on her way to the fridge, when in through the front door walks Henry. I was so fucked up last night, he lets everyone know. I am so hung-over, he elaborates as he opens the fridge. He eyes Frances walking over and says, looking for this? He holds up the beer and swings it alluringly back and forth, tempting her to grab it from his hands. Then he quickly twists off the cap and raises the bottle to his lips. Frances looks at Henry about to drink. Then she looks over at Bug who is watching Henry the way a hungry dog watches a bone. Then she looks at Ryan, and he is looking at her, a little smile on his lips. Frances turns back to Henry and they all watch as he takes a long, deep swallow.

BUFFALO
Cancelled

I don't want to talk about it.

.

THE CHARIOT OF YOUR MOTHER'S NEIGHBOURS' GODS

At the time, it is often hard to see where it all goes right, or wrong, and it is only later that these things become clear. For Bug it may have been the agreement reached with his mother that while she was away vacationing in Wild Wood, N. J. he would stay at her apartment, feed the cats, watch cable, swim morning laps in the pool, etcetera. Or it may have been the decision not to leave the party, to tell his friends good-bye, to take that second tab of acid and follow some girl into some room, lose her in the next, lose something else in the third, and the fourth, and the fifth, and find himself wandering the streets aimlessly till finally, lo and behold, somehow there is King Edward Avenue, and the line of familiar houses, and halfway down the block, his mother's apartment building.

The last of the night air blows soft and sweet. Stars still glimmer in the brightening sky. One of them catches Bug's eye, and he watches as it moves quickly from the horizon, toward the sleepy city, then straight down the middle of King Edward, stopping some ten feet in front of him. It is a mid-sized object – approximately the same dimensions as a Toyota Camry station wagon – that glows in a swirl of colours much like those photos you see of Uranus, or Bug wonders, is that Neptune? Before he can answer this question, a door of some type opens in the Camry object and two forms step onto the road. Bug's knees buckle, and he starts a collapse toward the hard asphalt, but is halted mid-fall by one of the forms, who, in less than an instant, is at his side, arms gentling holding him, warm voice saying, don't worry Bug, I have you.

– What . . . what are you?

– We are you, answers the other form now also standing close. This form looks like a man, but not like any man Bug has ever met.

– I am John, says this new man.

– And I am Theresa, says the form holding Bug who is turning to see what looks like a woman, though a woman like no other he has ever seen. We are from the future, she continues while still cradling Bug's shaking body, come, let us sit on the trunk of the car, have a beer, and you can collect your thoughts, as we realize this must be startling for you.

Bug, John and Theresa rest on their car, beers are passed around, and Theresa lights Bug's cigarette. The car door is open and from the inside comes the most heavenly sounds. John and Theresa stare off peacefully into the fading night. Conversation is slow to start. Bug breaks the ice. So, what is this we're listening to? he asks.

– Ahh, says John, that is the Bee Thousand album recorded by the Guided By Voices.

– The rock band, from Dayton? asks Bug.

– The very same.

– I know that band, says Bug and though his brain is startled and strained by the pace of incredible events he is still able to point out to his new friends, and I don't think they have a record called Bee Thousand.

– Yes, we know, they will not record the album until the year 1994.

– Remember we are from your future, adds Theresa, from the year 3023.

– But that's like more than a thousand years from now, observes Bug.

– Yes, we know, she answers.

– So how do you know Guided By Voices? I mean, there's no way they ever get that famous, is there?

– Yes there is, explains John, but not as you might imagine. After the hostile take-over of the united world government by the allied forces of business the followers of democracy were driven into hiding. It was a dark, dark time for mankind. Corporations fronted by human puppets roamed the planet in search of markets and profits. Deep underground the remaining human beings began their struggle, and they took their inspiration from the last instance in recorded human history when small groups of people had banded together and fought for something other than gross receipts, from the final time human beings believed in something more than money, from the fabled indie-rockers of the late twentieth century.

– The mighty struggle lasted for five hundred years, continues Theresa, until the great battle of Lake Winnipeg, in which the armies of men finally defeated the various marauding business concerns, the corporate veil was fatally pierced, and the evil multinationals were wound down forever. And through those five hundred long, hard years the songs of the fabulous forgotten played everywhere free men and women struggled.

– It is ironic to us who now live in a world of peace and love, adds John, where each gives according to his abilities and takes according to her needs, that all the great figures of your age, your various kings and presidents, generals and sporting stars, television idols and new media billionaires, all these mighty ones have long since been consigned to the dustbin of history, and now not even the eldest and most learned of our people can recall their once-feared names, while the days and deeds of your McCaughans and Moulds, your Deals, Does and Dandos roll off the tongues of even the smallest children.

– Wow, says Bug, that is ironic. Then he wonders aloud, is there any more beer?

– Silly Bug, answers Theresa, in the future there is always more beer. And as she passes him a fresh can, her fingers brush against his, dance lightly, then her arm slips around his waist, and she kisses him hard on the mouth. Before Bug knows what has happened, Theresa's robe is open, and she is spread across the hood of the car, and she has four breasts, and each is firmer and hotter than the one before, and a snow-white stomach leads to the valley of milk and honey between her legs, and Bug is gently moving in, past trembling lips, and she is slowly pinching her upper left nipple, pulling his mouth to it, when he remembers to ask . . . ahh, is John cool with this?

– Don't worry dear Bug, Theresa answers, in the future we all love each other. And with that settled, her steely nipple darts into his mouth. Bug pulls lovely soft future breast along with it, and pushing into her he feels something pushing into him. Bug turns, and over his shoulder is John, also disrobed, and standing right behind him. We'll just put the head in, he says, and if you

176

don't like it, we'll talk about it. Bug nods and smiles, then turns back to Theresa. He slides deep inside her, and at the same time feels John sliding deep inside him, and Bug has never felt anything quite like this before. He is fucking her and he is fucking him and she is fucking him and the car is rocking and the tape is playing and it goes on and on and on and at the end of the street a shimmer of light begins and it ripples toward them, as if a pebble has been thrown into the pond of time and space, and as those ripples pass familiar houses, pass his mother's apartment, they leave a path of glowing white erasing everything that has ever been before, and as it comes up on the car he is exploding into her exploding into him exploding into them and Bug has never felt anything anywhere near these super novas of cum erupting through mountains of cocaine into skies of clear acid ass pumping fantastic and it is so hot so white so hard so Bug could care so less about the may be rights could be wrongs, because he has seen the future, and it is better than what has come before, though he will never know that for sure, because the next morning when his eyes finally open he does not remember much about when it began, or ended, or even if it ever was, because all he really knows is the pool of vomit on the lawn by his cement sticky mouth, the pants around ankles, tacky cum on hand and thighs, left thumb up his ass, and Mrs. Aiken, from 10C, staring, with her small dog Randolph, back-lit by the Sunday sun.

SYRACUSE

The Round House

Yeah, well apparently there are worse things for a show to be than can-celled. The high point of my evening comes as I am putting away the gear and one of the house roadies asks if I have a light for his cigarette, and I go, yeah your face my ass, and he just kind of looks at me, but then he doesn't know that my friend Ryan used to love that gag when we were kids, when someone would ask for a match, and you would say the my ass yr face bit, but he only loved it when someone asked for a light. There was something about getting that joke wrong, that he just couldn't get enough of. We used to laugh so hard about stuff like that, about anything really.

THE MEN FROM GLAD

Small clouds of dirt and paper are stirred up when they pull away from the curb, it's hot and the bus is crowded. Though it's a Tuesday afternoon, and he's worked a full day sweatshirt folding, Ryan is still quite hung over. As they stop and start he is bumped into the woman next to him. He gives an embarrassed smile to show he is not trying for the cheap thrill, and then looks out the window at the buildings and cars and people, and man is it hot.

Thankfully his stop is next, and so he starts to make his way toward the doors. An old woman in front is having trouble with her bags. She can't seem to get her fingers through the handles. Ryan waits as she pulls it together. Then there are other problems: the man ahead of them doesn't want to move; hey, c'mon buddy, Ryan says to him, and buddy pretends to shift out of the way; the old woman is squeezing by his fat ass, and Ryan is wanting to punch him in the face, when a commotion begins behind them; Ryan looks back to see a big man with red hair cut short, wearing a pair of glasses with thick lenses, his right elbow is high in the air and he is using it to push his way through the crowd, fucking people, he is saying, fucking, cocksucking people; up front the doors open, the old woman makes her way out, and they follow her through.

On the sidewalk Ryan sees why the red haired man was only using the one arm, behind him he is dragging a young girl. Paying no attention he lifts her off the last step, and for a moment she dangles in the air like a broken kite, before he sets her down on the sidewalk. He lets go of her arm and still cursing walks off down the street. She trails a few feet behind in her cheap print dress and old sneakers with pictures of Saturday morning cartoon stars, looking in the store windows. The old woman from the bus is there beside Ryan and together they watch them go. Ryan shrugs when the old woman looks at him shaking her head . . . what are you going to do?

A postcard from Stephen is waiting at home, a picture of a pyramid or something, in Egypt or someplace. Will takes a quick look at the back but doesn't actually read it, somehow not in the mood for news from someone else's wonderful life. Dropping the card he heads for the bathroom. Clothes fall in a pile on the floor. Ryan opens the faucets. Covered in soap, he thinks about a girl, then decides not to; instead, he turns the cold on full and lets it run for as long as he can take it. The towel he puts to his face is still damp from this morning and smells bad. Back in his room, he opens the laundry hamper and starts to pack the dirty clothes into an old hockey bag. He enjoys going to the laundromat. It brings a little order and purpose to the day. Week. Month. Year. When he's done with the hamper he pulls the sheets off his bed and puts them in too. Then he gets the detergent and fabric softener out from under the sink. On the way down the hall he remembers the towel and the clothes in the bathroom and grabs them as well.

The laundromat is five blocks. There is another that's only three, but Ryan is no longer their customer. None of the machines work, it smells, and they don't lock it up at night; it just stays open. Sure, he went there at first. It was closer, and he liked that it was open all night, but the vague scent of urine always bothered him, and the machines really didn't work: sometimes your clothes came out soaking wet; other times with thick globs of detergent stuck to them; and then there were times you put your money in and not a goddamn thing happened. After a couple of experiences like that Ryan got wise and started walking the extra two blocks.

His laundromat has plate glass windows. LAVORAMA is painted on the front in large red letters. Underneath it says COLD & HOT WATER WASHERS, CHEAPEST TUMBLE-DRY IN TOWN, etc. Inside there is a wooden bench running parallel to the front window. In the corner where the bench ends there is a payphone, and some vending machines, one for coffee, one for soft drinks, another for detergent, bleach, and fabric softener. In the middle of the room there are three rows of washing machines. In the back a folding table runs between two walls of industrial dryers. There are also a few giant washing machines for sleeping bags, drapes, and other larger items. Ryan puts his bag down and opens a pair of machines, one for whites, and one for darks. The summer has wasted along this way, drunk at a bar most nights, tired and working most days, the rest of the time spent alone, watching television, reading detective novels, a blankness settling in him, on everything he sees.

Midway through sorting his clothes, Ryan notices a broke-down guy who seems to have suddenly appeared by the payphone. He is standing very still not making a sound. He has one foot on the bench, and his pant leg has pulled up. Ryan can see the broke-down guy's sock, it is red, the kind you might wear with a suit, but old and stretched out of shape, his shoes are taped up, hair long and greasy.

Quarters are pushed in and the washing machines rumble to life. Ryan takes a seat, starts reading his book. Lifting his eyes, he can see that the broke-down guy has this routine going. He stands by the bench, with his foot up, looking out the window. Then he goes and checks the coin returns in the payphone and the vending machines. After this he walks to the back, around the folding tables a couple of times, then he goes into the bathroom and closes the door. After about half a minute he comes out, walks to the front, puts his foot up on the bench again, and looks out the window. This happens every five minutes or so.

Ryan continues on with his reading. The book is OK, it's not too dull, about a sheriff, in a town somewhere, and everything is easy and then everything is going to hell. Ryan is at the part where everything is going to hell when he hears someone walk into the laundromat. Looking up he sees the red-haired man from the bus, with his laundry in a couple of garbage bags slung over his shoulder. He drops the bags to the ground, then walks over to the change machine, pulls a handful of wrinkled bills out of his pocket, and starts trying to stuff a crumpled old bill in backwards . . . cocksucking, motherfucking thing, I'll show you, you little cocksucker, son of a whore, cunt, I'll show you, just get in there. Ryan picks up his chair and goes outside, the light coming through the window strong enough to read by. He opens his book, and then, against his better judgment, peeks over his shoulder: the broke-down guy is standing perfectly still, hands held high in mid air, and he reminds Ryan of a statue, of a faun, in a garden; behind the faun the red-haired man stumbles around like a retarded zombie from an old fashion movie. There but for the grace of god, goes Ryan with a chuckle; though, if anyone had been there to share his little joke, they may have noted the chuckle was also little, and bitter. Ryan drops his eyes back to the page where things continue to go downhill for the sheriff.

When he heads back in to check on his laundry, the broke-down guy is just beginning his rounds. He starts at the coin slots, and then makes his way back towards the dryers. There is a pile of clothes on the folding table, and three empty Cokes in a line. The red-haired man is at the vending machine starting in on his fourth can, and watching the broke-down guy circle around the table . . . hey, what the . . . hey cocksucker . . . yeah you, you greasy haired cocksucker, what the fuck are you doing over there? What the fuck are you looking at you greasy haired cocksucker, get the hell away from there. The red-haired man starts walking towards the folding table. Cocksucker, he says, what're you looking at? Are you looking at my daughter's dainties? Are you looking at my daughter's dainties you sorry son of a bitch? What're you looking at? You're looking at my daughter's goddamn dainties!

The broke-down guy stares at him and doesn't say a thing. The red-haired man keeps coming on, talking that way. The broke-down guy just stands there. He doesn't move or say anything. The red-haired man shoves him backward against a dryer. You cocksucking pervert, he says, I'll show you, looking at little girl's underwear. I'll show you, you goddamn greasy haired pervert. Then the red-haired man hits the broke-down guy right in the middle of the face. The broke-down guy falls, in a pile, to the ground. The red-haired man stands over him, his back to Ryan, and it is pervert bastard this and greasy cocksucker that.

Ryan is beside a row of chairs thinking: I should pick one up and hit the son of a bitch; if he goes for him again, I will hit him, if he makes the move I will grab a chair and hit him; he will go for him, and then I will hit him on the back of the head with a chair; he will fall down, and his glasses will break, and there will be blood on his face. Ryan is thinking: someone else would have hit him already, someone else would have hit the son of a bitch by now, Joe Strummer would have hit the son of a bitch; come on, you useless motherfucker, hit him, now is the time not be one more useless motherfucker. And as he is thinking all this old familiar feelings swirl: his hands are shaking, and sweat is pouring through his skin, soaking his clothes; inside he feels the white hot static electric; the pins and needles fire in his fingers, his heart, his head; the breath is coming much too fast, much too shallow. And then the red-haired man pulls his leg back and kicks. He kicks quick and hard, and it sounds like his foot is hitting a bag of wet shit. Then he lifts the broke-down guy by an arm and a leg and carries him by Ryan – so close that he could have touched them – and out the door. The broke-down guy lies on the ground where he gets dropped. Ryan watches the red-haired man walk back inside. His mouth is still going and he is wiping his hands together like he has just finished building a tree house. His face is covered with sweat and he is walking around near the payphone . . . cocksuckers doing dirt. Goddamn perverts everywhere. Saw him, just like that, plain as fucking day, saw what he was doing, they can't fool me, can't fool me, I saw him . . .

Ryan starts pulling his still wet stuff out of the dryers and throwing it into his hockey bag. He doesn't look up, but can hear the man with the red hair moving around near the bathroom, mouth always going. Ryan keeps his head down as he makes for the front doors, steps out into the night, and doesn't look back. The broke-down guy is still there on the sidewalk. His legs are crossed and he is watching the traffic. The sun has set bruising the sky dark purple. Ryan says, hey, you alright? He walks over. You OK? Ryan says again. C'mon, you should get out of here, and tries to slip his hands under broke-down's arms, to help him up, but is shaken off. Broke-down stands up by himself, and then seems to notice Ryan for the first time. He looks at Ryan for a moment, brushes the lapels of his jacket, then turns his back and walks away . . . Ryan knows what to do; go home and turn on the TV and drink.

KINGSTON
Alfie's

Well, well, well, finally back in Canada. The home of the free, land of
the brave, and best of all, only two more shows, because I'm tired,
maybe I'm too old for this stuff, maybe twenty-seven is too old for this,
sitting in the hotel thinking these sad little thoughts, drinking from a
big happy bottle, looking at Courtney Love on the television talking
about that crap movie where she played a stripper-junkie, you know,
the one where we're supposed to believe that the greatest threat to free
speech in the whole wide world is some rightwing religious nut-case,
and not the planet dominating mass media control everything we see
read hear corporation who made the dumb piece of shit in the first
place, then she goes on about what she's gonna wear to the Oscars,
and how Sharon Stone is lending her this really great dress, and how
she is all excited about that, and everyone gives the hippies a hard
time, but at least it took them twenty-five years to turn into irrelevant
assholes, seems our rock heroes can do it over a long weekend, what-
ever, I guess the joke's on us, and I guess they're just doing what we'd
all do if we ever got even half the chance, and I guess who really cares
anyway, cause that whole rock hero thing was a crap idea in the first
place, and I guess I get drunker, call Gidget, get her machine, mention
we will be in Toronto tomorrow, at the El Mocombo, and I'll put her
on the list, if she happens to be in the neighbourhood, with some time
to kill.

THE WOMEN'S MOVEMENT

Forty below, Henry is standing in a phone booth, at four a.m., on the wrong side of town. It's almost too much to slip the quarter into the slot. The number pads feel like ice cubes. It rings once, twice, three times, then a sleepy voice says hello. Frances, he says, hey Frances, it's me.

A hellish two blocks and he is on her doorstep knocking hard. OK, OK, she says as she opens up. In the kitchen she pours him a cup of tea. Her hair is messy. She is wearing sweatpants and an old flannel shirt that Henry recognizes as one of his. She puts the cup in front of him and then says, are you OK?

– Oh yeah.

– You sounded awful on the phone.

– It's cold out there.

– Like you were in trouble.

– I'm not in trouble.

– So, you're OK?

– Yeah, OK.

– OK, then what are you doing?

– What am I doing?

– Here, what are you doing *here*?

– Visiting.

– Henry, you are not allowed to visit.

– So, that's it? he says to her, that's what it's come to, can't even stop by to say hello anymore?

– It's four a.m. . . . . you're drunk . . .

– What do you mean?

– What do you think I mean?

– Believe me, I haven't got a clue.

– You came here to try and get laid.

– No I didn't.

– And that is sad.

– No it's not, because I didn't.

– You didn't come here to get laid?

– No, but if you want to think that I came here to get laid, if that is what you think, if that is what you are thinking about, well then . . .

– Shut up.

Her shirt is buttoned low and Henry catches a glimpse of her bra. He remembers that bra. It's green, with bits of lace, and wires underneath. He wonders if she is wearing the matching underwear. Half-cut, like a pair of little gym shorts, but thin, with the lace, and he is starting to get a bit of a hard-on, when in walks her roommate Angie. Is everything all right? she yawns.

– Yeah, says Frances, sorry about the noise.

– Evening Angie.

– How are you doing Henry? she asks as she pushes a piece of hair back from her face, it's been a while.

– Yeah, it has. I'm good. Real good, thanks. And you?

– Henry was just leaving, interrupts Frances.

– Leaving? he asks.

– Going home.

– I have no cab money, the buses are finished, it's impossible.

– You can walk, says Frances.

– Home? In this weather? Forced out, like the Eskimos, with their grandparents, on the pieces of ice, to die, it's not right.

– There's plenty of room on the couch, says Angie. Frances and Angie look at each other for a second. OK, I guess you can stay on the couch, says Frances. Great, I can stay on the couch, Henry confirms. Angie smiles, well, since that's all settled . . .

-Good night, he says. Night Henry, she disappears down the hall. He turns to Frances and says, I always thought she didn't like me.

– She doesn't like you Henry. She's my friend. None of my friends like you. She's just being decent. You should try it sometime.

– You're right, he says, I don't know what's wrong with me. Turning up like this. I'm so fucked up, he confides.

– Well, hopefully you'll feel better in the morning, says Frances as she goes to the closet. She gets a pillow and some blankets, and then heads into the next room. In here, she says and Henry follows. She lays the pillow and blankets down on the couch. You can watch TV, she says, just keep it down. Sitting on the couch he asks, you want to smoke pot? Frances looks at Henry for a long moment and then says, no thanks. In response, he looks at her for his own moment. What happened to us, he asks, I used to dream about us Frances. About us getting married, having a house, kids. And what happened to all that?

– Are you fucking kidding me?

– No, I am not, I am not fucking kidding you, I had dreams Frances, dreams.

– You really don't get it, do you? She shakes her head and finishes with, Good night Henry. She walks to the door, stops for a moment. I'm going to Paris, at the end of this semester, for a year, she says, I got into the Sorbonne.

– Wow congratulations, that's really great, I'm so proud of you, says Henry, so what's the Sorbonne? Frances laughs, then comes back and gives him a tight hug, and then she's gone, the door closing behind her.

Henry smokes pot, flips through the channels, but there is nothing on. He turns off the TV. It's dark in the room. Staring up at the ceiling he thinks about Frances, thinks about her going, thinks her shirt was unbuttoned pretty low, and she did hug me, thinks she thinks I don't get it, but she's the one that doesn't get it. I know her. I remember her perched on the bathroom sink, while her mom watched TV in the next room. And I remember my cock in her ass, in the park, by the fountain, on a warm spring night. I know the truth about her. We're the same, and always will be, there is a dark scar on both of us. And even if we don't want it, we still want it. In fact, that just makes us want it more. A hot, dark scar that you keep secret from everyone else, but you touch it when you are alone. And I'm touching it now. And I know she is too. I know she is in her room touching herself like I've seen her do so many times before.

Quietly he steps out into the hall, walks past the bathroom, and then stops outside Frances' door. He thinks, Reach out! Open the door! To have what you want! Not what you should want, what you really want. And to get that all you need to do is ask. Most people spend their whole lives wanting, when all you have to do is ask. It's that easy. We all want it. We all know we all want it. What are we waiting for. So Henry puts his ear to the door. And there is her muffled voice, so soft he almost misses the oh yeah, yeah, yeahs . . . I knew it, celebrates Henry, I knew it because that is how people really are. They stand up straight and say what they think they should, but when the lights go out, and it's late at night, and the door is closed, they dream of what they really want. Henry keeps his ear to the door. Frances keeps purring, oh yeah, oh yeah, oh yeah, and he thinks of her kneeling on the bed, like he's seen so many times, ass lifted, pussy up, hand between legs, rubbing, dreaming of what they both want. So he doesn't think anymore, he does, and he pushes open the door, and he sees what he had thought, Frances from behind, her ass up in the air, and she is rubbing her pussy, but there is something else. Angie is kneeling at the edge of the bed, with a dildo in her hand, that she is pushing into Frances. And though Frances' face is buried in a pillow, with the door open Henry can now clearly hear oh yeah, oh yeah, yeah, yeah, yeah . . .

He closes the door. It was only opened for a second but the image lingers in front of his eyes, like spots left from staring at the sun. He stands there quiet, praying they didn't notice, straining his ears for any clue. From the other side of the door he hears Angie say, you like that, don't you? Henry doesn't think they noticed. He stands there for a bit more. There are so many things that he is thinking: Frances is a lesbian! A lesbian! And if she is not a lesbian, then at least bi! And she is fucking Angie! How long has this been going on? Was she a lesbian when I was with her? Was she bi? How come I never knew about this? How come we never did it with another girl? But mostly he is thinking about two girls, on the other side of the door, one of them bent over, the other pushing a dildo into her pussy. It being Frances aside, this is probably the most exciting thing that has ever happened to Henry. The thing he has wanted the most, in his whole wide life, is now happening inches away. He nudges the door open. Through the crack he looks at the girls. They are in the same position. Angie is pushing hard and deep. Frances starts the low, steady whine of pleasure that Henry knows will lead to her climax. He slips his hand into his boxers and grabs hold of his cock, but is surprised to find that he is not that hard. It takes a few pulls to stiffen. And he never quite gets there. In fact, it's still a bit soft when he cums. And he only cums a little, which is also not at all what he had expected. The many nights spent imagining something like this, he had always thought he'd be rock hard, and spurting summer volcanoes, but it isn't like that.

On the bed Frances turns over. Henry watches them move slowly together and kiss, bodies sweetly singing each to each. He closes the door and walks back down the hall to the living room. He sits down on the couch and pulls a blanket around him. A streetlight shines in through the window. Ice fingers stretch out across the glass.

TORONTO
El Mocambo

Gidget doesn't show. I take my time putting away the gear, just in case she's late. Still working on it when they close the bar. The staff's all downstairs, and I'm wrapping the last of the cables when I notice Phil sitting at a table, at the back, in the dark. Have you been there the whole time? Yeah, he says. I think about mentioning, well maybe you could have helped load out, you lazy bastard, but decide against it. You want a drink? Sure, and I take a seat at the table. We sit sipping not talking. After a bit Phil starts, I saw Stiff Little Fingers here when I was fourteen. Hitchhiked all the way from Montreal. Only time the original band toured North America. They played for more than two and a half hours. Played everything, Alternative Ulster, Nobody's Hero, Suspect Device, Gotta Get Away, all the hits. The place was packed and people were just going crazy. I was right at the front, could have reached out and touched Jake Burns. The last song he says, this is an old Irish folk song, and then they do a cover of Teenage Kicks . . . changed my life forever. We finish the bottle not saying much else, but I know we're both thinking the same things: every crap show we ever played for no money, every shit band that ever made it bigger than us cause they were smarter and we were stupider, and they cared more and we cared less, about all the wrong things. I look at Phil sitting scared, lonely and forgotten and it's all I can do not to lean over and kiss him. Instead we finish the whole bottle, then almost fall down the stairs break our necks. Phil has somewhere to go so I walk back to the hotel along deserted streets. Never felt so all alone in all my life. Till I open the hotel doors and there is Gidget sitting in the lobby. Just like in some dumb movie. Continuing on in that vein, we go to an all night donut coffee place, sit there talking till the sun comes up

WE'VE GOT THE BEATIFIC

Ryan likes to drive when he's high. The car feels like a spaceship. He feels like a friendly alien as he steers around a corner. Houses full of happy earthlings glide by. Henry changes the tape and puts on the Pixies, *Doolittle*.

– Not again, Ryan groans.

– Why not? Why not again? It's a great album.

– I agree, but every time we get in the car it's *Doolittle*. It's like air, I can't even hear it anymore. At least play a different Pixies record.

– But *Doolittle* is their masterpiece, he says.

Ryan starts to argue for *Surfer Rosa*, and they talk and talk as the houses slide by, but Henry isn't having any of it. They have been smoking hashish sprinkled with cocaine for the last few hours, so it is pretty easy for them to find the words. There's even a lot to be said for *Bossa Nova*, Ryan tells him, but Henry isn't listening anymore. He is playing with something. What's that? asks Ryan his eyes still, more or less, on the road.

– Nothing, Henry answers as he unrolls his window.

– Close that, it's fucking freezing.

– OK. Henry has his arm out the window and suddenly there is a loud, flat pop and a mailbox just to the left of the car jerks and falls over dead.

– ARE YOU OUT OF YOUR MOTHERFUCKING MIND?

– DRIVE!

– ARE YOU OUT OF YOUR MOTHERFUCKING MIND?

– DRIVE!

– ARE YOU OUT OF YOUR MOTHERFUCKING MIND?

– FUCKING DRIVE!

But Ryan is already fucking driving, the old Nova's engine groaning as he floors it up the hill. PIECE OF SHIT GO FASTER, he commands. YOUR CAR IS A PIECE OF SHIT, he tells Henry. At the corner he turns right, then left, left, right driving aimlessly until he is sure that there is no one to lose. Ryan parks the car then turns to Henry.

– Was that a gun? Did you just shoot a fucking gun?

– Maybe.

– You are so fucked. So totally and completely fucked.

– You should have seen your face. That was funny. I wish you could've seen the look on your face. Henry is laughing very hard.

– Fuck you.

– It was a joke.

– It wasn't funny.

– Oh come on, don't be like that.

– You are a stupid dick, says Ryan lighting a cigarette, I almost had a fucking heart attack.

– Sorry . . . you want to hold it?

– Fuck no. Ryan takes a couple of drags. Here, let me see that. Henry hands it over. Careful, it's loaded, he says. Ryan takes it in his hand. The gun is still warm.

– Is this real?

– Of course it's real.

– Where did you get it?

– Found it at work. In Terry's desk drawer. This morning. I was looking for a drink. Pretty cool, isn't it?

– No, it's not pretty cool. It's a fucking gun, and Terry is going to shit, then make you eat it when he finds out. He'll never know, answers Henry as he mimes Terry too drunk to notice a thing. Ryan hands it back to Henry. You are definitely fucking losing it, he tells him and then counsels, I am not fucking kidding, you need to get some help. Ryan turns on the car and starts to drive.

They park by the store. Henry goes in for beer. Tired of the car, Ryan stretches his legs, sits on a nearby bench, listens to the gears spin in his head, smoke-filled thoughts propelled by burnt powders, watches the snow falling gently through the blue night, when suddenly all is startled by a kid who has stopped, and is now standing right in front of him staring. What do you want kid, asks Ryan.

– You don't remember me, do you?

– What?

– Chris, from the rink, when that dad got hit in the head.

– What?

– The outdoor rink, like three four years ago, your friend hit some dad with a slap shot, we all went running over, the little kid on the toboggan, remember?

– Oh yeah, yeah, right, how you been?

– Good. How about you?

– Awesome, I've been pretty much awesome.

– You sure?

– Sure I'm sure. Why wouldn't I be sure?

– Nothing . . . and just then Henry comes back with the beer. He looks at the kid. He looks at Ryan. Who's the kid?

– Chris, from when you hit that guy in the head, at the rink.

– Wow, blast from the past, says Henry, you want a beer Chris?

– No, I got to go meet some friends.

– OK, well take care then, says Ryan.

– Yeah, don't do anything I wouldn't do, says Henry.

Chris looks at them funny, says OK, see you, and walks off. After a few feet he stops and turns, Hey, I made the team.

– Fantastic, says Henry, what team?

– St. Kevin's, he says but now he is looking at, speaking only to Ryan, just like we were talking about that day, I made the team. The kid and Ryan look at each other for a long minute; then the kid turns, starts walking away and doesn't look back. Ryan watches him disappearing into the snow. Kid's weird, says Henry.

They push open the Bar doors, Ryan heads straight for the hard stuff, trying to put his thoughts in order, and is not much good for conversation. Henry drifts off to chat up a girl. He becomes quite engrossed, doesn't pay much attention when Ryan tells him he needs the keys, that he left something in the car, so Henry hands them over quickly, and then turns back to her. Ryan gets in the car and starts to drive.

The part that he liked best, what he really loved, was that moment standing in front of the gate, as the Zamboni made its final sweep, and then that first step out onto the ice, the silver song of a sharp blade, the puck ringing off the boards, the symphony of skates as they started their warm-up. The wall behind the stands was made of frosted glass and when the sun shone through on a Saturday morning the rink filled with a shimmering light. And the smell, there is no place on earth that smells like a hockey rink. Ice. Wood. Metal. Leather. Sweat. And that one elusive final ingredient, the scent of Zamboni, a cold clean smell from the future, a smell of hope, of games yet to be played, of fresh untouched ice, of all of your tomorrows.

The parking lot is around back of the church. Ryan slides into a spot and kills the engine. The lights are off in the rectory. He opens the glove compartment and takes the gun out. It's cold and heavy. He cradles it in his lap, then opens the chamber and looks at the bullets resting like little babies in their cribs. He snaps it shut, places the gun to his head, and thinks this is the time, the do or die, the him or me, the death; and he thinks about the things that had happened, and the things that were happening, and the things that were going to happen; and he waits for the fear. The seconds creak into minutes, his breath holds calm and steady, blowing small white clouds through his lips to the dashboard, and the fear never comes. Ryan opens the driver's side, steps into the blue winter night.

Father Tom answers the door in a dressing gown. His face is clouded by sleep. Cheeks grey with stubble. Yes? he says his voice puzzled and thick.

– Hello Tom.

– Can I help you? he says peering out into the night, trying to place the face. Ryan raises the gun and points it. Tom steps back into the hallway and Ryan follows him in. The lights are on, and Ryan can see recognition spread across the old, worn features.

– Ryan, my God, what are you doing here?

– You know, Tom.

– Money, is it money . . . ?

– Oh come on, you know.

– I heard you started with the drugs, but . . .

– Tell me why I'm here, Tom.

– I have no idea.

– Tell me why. And to move the conversation along, Ryan cocks the gun.

– Jesus Ryan, please.

– Tell me why.

– Ryan don't . . .

– YOU TELL ME WHY I AM HERE!

– It's only because I loved you, so much, I'm so sorry, so very sorry. You don't know how long I've wanted to apologize, ask for your forgiveness, how hard it's been . . .

– That's nice Tom, Ryan stops him, but not exactly why I'm here. Then he cracks the old man in the side of the head with the gun butt.

– Sweet Jesus, he says stumbling back against the wall. He slides down to the floor where he starts to sob, I was sick, I love you, I need help . . . Ryan points the gun at this head that keeps sobbing. He keeps it pointed for a long time, but he doesn't shoot. He looks at the man on the floor and he cannot shoot. He tries with all his heart but cannot, and he doesn't know why. All he knows is he cannot make the finger squeeze the trigger. Tom, he says, I need to use the bathroom.

– What?

– The bathroom, Tom. I need to use the bathroom. Get up, you're coming too.

The bathroom is off the long, narrow hall that leads to the bedroom. The bedroom has no window and the hall is the only way out. Ryan remembers all this. In a horrible way, it's a bit like coming home. He directs Tom to the bedroom and tells him to sit on the bed. Tells him if he tries to leave, he will be seen, and he will be shot. Ryan goes to the bathroom and sits on the edge of the bathtub. Over the sink there is a picture of Jesus.

– What am I going to do? asks Ryan, I should kill him. I know it's wrong, but I should. Jesus does not say anything.

– He deserves it, Ryans continues, come on, he deserves to die, don't you think? Jesus still doesn't say anything.

– And if I don't, what'll happen then. I mean, what are you going to do about all this shit? Jesus remains tight-lipped.

– OK, well, we all know your position on these things, Ryan tells him, but sometimes there are some people who really deserve it, and that's just the way it is. Jesus stares at Ryan. Ryan stares back. There is not much left to talk about.

Tom is still sitting on the edge of the bed. Ryan looks around the room. Doesn't this remind you of old times Tom? he says.

– Ryan please . . .

– SHUT! THE FUCK! UP! Don't you say a fucking word. Now take off your robe. TAKE IT FUCKING OFF!

The robe falls to the floor and there is his fat middle-aged body. Ryan crosses the room and stands in front of him.

– Well, well, this really is like old times.

– Ryan . . .

– NOT! A! FUCKING! WORD!

Ryan takes the barrel of the gun and runs it over Tom's lips, down to his chest, across his belly, till he reaches his cock. Tom starts to get an erection. Ryan sticks the muzzle into his gut and kneels in front of him. Don't fucking move, he tells him. Ryan starts to give him head, and Father Tom is starting to like it, he's liking it a lot, and he is starting with his little throat noises, and they get louder and Ryan knows Tom is getting close. The balls tighten up and the cock starts to jump. Ryan stands up fast and takes a step back. Tom's eyes pop open. The gun is pointed right at his chest.

– DIE MOTHERFUCKER DIE, yells Ryan as he squeezes the trigger, all the while looking into the old familiar face. He sees the surprise and he sees the fear, but what he doesn't see is the body jerk backward, or bullets tear through flesh and bone, or the blood seep out and the life pass away. And what he hears is click, click, clickclickclickclickclickclickclick . . . click . . . the gun being empty, Ryan having taken the bullets out.

The room is now very quiet. Ryan is looking into the eyes that thought they were about to die. And that will have to be enough. So he soaks it in, trying to make the moment last, but a funny thing happens. That look of surprise and fear does not stop. It just gets stronger. Tom's breath starts to come in deep rasps, and he claws at his chest. Then a wave of absolute terror breaks across his face. His eyes bulge out, his knees buckle and he falls back on the bed, his head and left arm hanging off the far edge. His cock is still erect. It jerks twice and then continues to bob as cum boils out. It is the only part of him moving. Ryan stands for a long time looking, but nothing else on him moves. Nothing there ever moves again.

At the front door is a large crucifix with Jesus hanging. As Ryan walks by it almost looks like Jesus is smiling down at him.

It almost looks like he wants to tell him, it's OK kid. It almost looks like he would like to lean down and pat Ryan on the back as he slips out the door; but of course Jesus doesn't, his hands being full.

Ryan steps out into the parking lot. It's morning. A soft, thick snow is falling. The world is perfectly quiet. He slides behind the wheel, steers the car up Regent, then left onto Sherbrooke. With every turn of the tires he is moving further away, but from what, and to where, it is hard to tell. All that's certain is that he is finally moving, that he is going, and that he is rolling down the window so he can call to his people, to all his sorry people, who don't know whether to laugh or cry, but know to keep quiet . . . Come on, my touched shaky brothers! Come on, my ill-caressed fat skinny sisters! We have nothing to left lose but our losing, put that cast iron dumbness down, don't you carry it one more slow sucking step. Meet me on the other side. Look, it is beautiful here, and look, you are beautiful here. Come on, we've wasted enough of everything already! Come on, there's nothing left to prove! Come on, come on, come on . . . and look, oh just look . . . as the car turns into that stream of blooming white, driving from this nowhere through to the next.

MONTREAL

Fou Foune Electronique

We come in through the maze of highway overpasses and off-ramps just like we've done a hundred times. There's the Mountain with St. Joseph's glowing on its side, and the lights of the city filling the sky, just like we've seen a thousand times. And you wished it felt good to be back home, but most of my friends are gone, so what's left? A bunch of buildings, a whole lot of strangers, and some places you used to know. That night at the club I stand at the back with my arm around Gidget watching them charge through the hits. It's good. The band. The night. To be with her. The club is packed. Henry shows up. It's funny, how all the time growing up we never really liked each other all that much. I mean, we liked each other, but we didn't really like each other. Now that we are the only ones left, we're the best of friends. It's funny how things turn out. Funny when you're kids. Funny when you're not. I introduce Henry to Gidget. We have a beer. Then we have another and Henry must be thinking similar thoughts because he suddenly says, here's to old friends. You can meet a lot of people in this life, do a lot of things, but old friends, the ones you grew up with, those little boys and girls, you can't ever meet them again, that can't happen ever again. He raises his bottle and says, so here's to Stephen and Ryan and Frances . . .and wherever those assholes are tonight, New York or London, Los Angeles, Tokyo or I don't give a fuck, I still love them, even though they're fucking quitters, and I can see little tears start in his eyes. He brushes them away and says, and I want you to know Bug . . . that I love you too . . . I really, really love you . . . kiss me Bug, and he tries to put his tongue in my mouth. He turns to Gidget and starts yelling, WE CAN SHARE HIM . . . YOU HAVE TO SHARE! I look at Gidget and shake my head. On stage the band is epic. Every song they're getting stronger and stronger. But as I stand there watching them I can't help but feel that this is the end. Sure, they might do it for another year, or another ten, but it's all over. Everybody knows, we just don't want to admit it, so we'll keep rocking out till the sun burns black. I order more drinks . . . scotch, for all my friends . . . Henry and me toast good-bye to our brand new era. Just then this little kid comes busting by. Nearly spills my drink. I'm saying, what the fuck? and Henry is laughing as I watch her and her boyfriend push their way to the front of the stage. Rude little fucks have their arms around each other, and they start jumping like retarded bunnies, and they don't stop. Up and down and up and down and pig tails little knapsacks and baggy pants flying till the very end. And after this they are going to steal their folks' car, drive all-night on cheap pills, and end up in some truck-stop at three a.m. ordering pie and coffee from the tired waitress while it rains outside. And when it's all done, after they crawl back home, and they kiss their moms on the cheek, they will lie in the dark under the covers and know that they'll never be the same again, and that's it. That's the best.

And we were at a later time moved to do well, after our hearts had conceived of Thy Spirit; but in the former time we were moved to do evil, forsaking Thee; but Thou, the One, the Good God, didst never cease doing good. And we also have some good works, of Thy gift, but not eternal; after them we trust in Thy great hallowing. But Thou, being the Good which needeth no good, art ever at rest, because Thy rest is Thou Thyself. And what man can teach man to understand this? or what Angel, an Angel? or what Angel, a man? Let it be asked of Thee, sought in Thee, knocked for at Thee; so, so shall it be received, so shall it be found, so shall it be opened. Amen.

—S. Augustine.